The Caged Bird's Delight

Blaise Monroe

Contents

Trigger Warnings

This book contains:

- blood and gore

- brief mentions of child abuse

- mental and physical abuse to adults

- sexual situations

- swearing

- violence (murder, torture, death, physical injuries)

Chapter 1 - Kalen

"How are we feeling today, Mr. Crowe?" The warden asks, pointedly looking at the fresh lacerations on my bare chest. His name is Grey. Or Goldilocks. Or, goddamn Joffrey, for all I know. It would be fitting for a sadistic, chronically-bored, power-hungry, blond little shit desperate to prove what a big man he is. He watches me silently with an irritating smile, tugging at his lips.

Like he's mocking me.

Like he knows something I don't.

Like he has me by the balls.

And maybe he does because I'm stuck in this damn cage, and what is his fucking *name*? I can't remember for the life of me. My memory's been trash lately. Moments of awareness flicker away as if they never were. The situations I've endured here are slowly eating away at the edges of my mind, my instincts, and my form. I inhale deeply, determined to retain what's left of my sanity.

I didn't become the leader of The Divide—an illicit organization that runs this city's underground —by avoiding blood, pain, or violence, but that was before my sentencing. After a month in ProMaxim prison, I'm beginning to feel the effects of prolonged physical exhaustion. If my brother Knox were here, he would remind me why I allowed myself to get caught in the first place. Why my sacrifice was necessary to help our people.

Those with Ankylos DNA aren't the only people I harbor and employ within The Divide—a name that represents those of us who are not quite human, not entirely alien but something in between — but us Ankylos are the race being disappeared. The ones being disproportionately sentenced to this very prison, disappearing without a trace under the watchful eyes of this very warden.

Things weren't always this way. My organization has managed to avoid detection for years, and the odd times we've had run-ins with the police, a handsome bribe always got them off our backs. But things changed five months ago when a couple of officers we'd never seen before, raided the casino we ran out of one of our multi-million dollar homes. Knox, my brother, and our friend Cameron were my right-hand men. At the time it was raided, Cameron was running the place. He bribed the officers, as per our protocol, but these new guys refused his offers. They didn't even make any arrests. They just shut the place down, ceased our assets, and took photos of everything, including Cameron.

I remember Cameron telling me he felt uneasy about the way things went down. It was unusual, and honestly, it troubled me, too. Knox and I instructed Cameron to stop working and just lay low since he grew paranoid about the incident. So he moved into one of my rental homes, but his paranoia worsened. Cameron called me every few days, claiming that unmarked cars were circling the block and driving slowly past the house. He believed it was those officers. I tried to reassure him that he was safe and we'd handle any shit that came his way together, despite thinking Cameron was losing it.

Knox and I would check on him often until he claimed to no longer see the strange cars in the neighborhood. It took Cameron a month to return to his old self, which allowed us to refocus on the business. Then, one day, Cameron went radio-silent and didn't answer my calls or texts. I was on my way to check on him when he called me from an unrecognizable number, telling me he'd been arrested by one of the officers who had raided our casino and that the warden had it out for him. He was taken to this very prison. Of course, I was livid. There was no trial. No lawyers - I could have paid for the best in town to represent him. It was essentially a glorified kidnapping.

Knox tried to visit him a few times, but the warden insisted there was no prisoner by that name. Months passed, and we never heard from Cameron again. We're completely convinced that this blond shitbag was directly involved in his disappearance.

And now that I'm here and can see the way things operate firsthand, I have a terrible feeling Cameron is dead.

More Ankylos have been sent to ProMaxim since we lost Cameron. I know it won't ever stop unless I investigate things for myself. I've sacrificed my freedom and safety to protect my own, and I would do it again in a heartbeat.

I stare defiantly into the cold, blue eyes of my tormentor, contrasted by his irritating smile.

My people only respect strength and determination, I remind myself. *There's no room for half-assed leadership. They depend on me to crawl out from under this warden's thumb, and liberate any of us I find. I can't allow myself to be broken by pain.*

This new affliction with my physical control and memory has everything to do with what this man has done to me. What he's still doing to me. And what he's likely been doing to others of my kind.

"Come on, Kalen," the warden begins in an amused tone, striding along the outside edge of my cell. It's strange to see someone so fragile attempt to wield power. "You have nothing to share? No mood swings or memory issues? No loss of appetite or physical changes?"

I watch his feet move, never crossing the threshold. He knows better than to step one foot inside and face me. It would only take one blow to break his vertebrae. Only a handful of steps separate us now. His eyes dart around the prison cell that encloses me as if he's aware of what I'm thinking. Then, his attention swivels back to me. I can tell he's looking for changes in my appearance or behavior, trying to figure out if or how I've been altered. But I would prefer he stop noticing me altogether.

I know slate-gray is an uncommon skin tone among humans, but for my kind, the Ankylos, it's one of three of the most common shades. Dark tan and light green are the other two. I'm sure he's studying the scales that cover the skin of my shoulders and throat with intrigue, but they are not new. My camouflage failed to mask them after the first week—a sign that I was under severe stress. A sign that his unethical experiments and tests are getting to me.

"Why don't you step in here and check for yourself?" I reply in a low voice.

"Oh, I'll check," he assures me, "when you aren't conscious, of course."

Though I try, my expression fails to obscure the sheer malice I possess for him. I had a feeling that I was being drugged. Sometimes, I'd awaken feeling slightly confused and nauseous, with a bandage on my forearms and soreness in that area like I'd had blood drawn. I tried to convince myself I was imagining things, but the warden's words were proof that all my suspicions were true. Instantly, a wave of disgust washes through me, and I feel sick. But I can't let him see this. He's looking for a reaction. I force myself to appear calm.

"Drugging me? On top of everything else. Surely that's a gross violation of my rights," I speak evenly. "A prison warden committing heinous crimes against hapless prisoners under his watch? I should report you." A menacing grin tugs at the corners of my lips, and my fangs are fully visible. "Maybe you'll land yourself in a cell right next to mine."

For a moment he looks shaken, brows raised and mouth agape, before he slips on a mask of cool indifference and smirks. "Somehow I doubt that. After all, you're not a protected class like your ancestors, nor like *humans* either. So, which rights have I violated exactly? Do mutants even have any?"

Ah, so that's how he justifies his crimes. I don't trust myself to say something I won't regret, so instead, I grit my teeth and say nothing.

Ankylos is not a pure alien race but a mixed race of people who are half-human and half-Drakon - an extraterrestrial Dragon race. They, along with a handful of other alien races, arrived on Earth in the early 1900s with the desire to collaborate with humans for genetic purposes. Governments across the world, desperate to obtain rare genetic material for use in their medical and military research, jumped at the opportunity to work with them. And so, the beings from the stars mated with humans, producing many offspring. Drakon, being the most ancient of the extraterrestrial races, possessed the most genetic diversity, which made their DNA the most valuable.

Over time, alien hybrids of all kinds mixed amongst each other and with humans, creating what some people referred to as "hybrids," "monsters," or the derogatory term "mutants." And, while the pure alien races were treated with utmost respect by human governments during their time on Earth, we, their hybrid offspring, couldn't say the same. In some parts of the world, we're deified and uplifted to the status of Gods. In other parts, we're merely tolerated at best, and at worst, we're treated like pariahs, facing hostility and discrimination.

Even though human and hybrid relations have improved over the past one hundred years, and we've managed to carve out our own place in society, we still find ourselves fighting to be seen as regular people. To be wholly accepted.

Goldilocks' eyes study the large curved horns that protrude from my head, a feature common in male Ankylos when they reach maturity. If I were a full-blooded Drakon, I would have vertical pupils, scales covering the entire length of my body, and possibly even a tail to match. But thanks to my Ankylos parents, heavens rest their souls, my human features are more pronounced. The warden's eyes trail lower, lingering on the clotting slashes across my body. I heal quickly, which he already knows because, like many hybrids, my alien lineage allows for regeneration. It's one of the reasons humans were willing to accept the existence of *aliens* at all. Opting to not only collaborate but cohabitate with non-humans was never a selfless choice. Alien DNA helped humans extend their lifespans by decades, bringing them closer to some alien races' natural life cycles of 200 years old. Without government-funded hybridization programs like Project Nexus, us hybrids would not exist.

Now, we cannot be unmade.

Suddenly, I realize I'm starving. Healing takes a lot of energy, and I wish I had one of those parmesan-crusted steaks with a side of fresh garlic mash. Or maybe a double-stacked carnivore burger from my kitchen. If only I could get my hands on a pot of—

"Must we do this every time?" The warden's exasperated question jolts me out of my thoughts, breaking the tense silence. It's not much, but it still pleases me to see that I've managed to piss him off a bit. "I simply want to know if you've experienced any changes, mentally or physically, in your opinion. Really, it's not a difficult question."

I keep quiet. Admit nothing.

Not the insomnia or anxiety caused by the constant stress and pain I'm made to endure, nor the depression that pulls me under whenever I think of Cameron, and many others who've been taken by this place. I won't tell him how disturbed I am by being drugged against my knowledge. Nor how the very mention of the Ice Room makes my throat tighten, and my blood run cold.

On the first night upon my arrival, I fell into an uncharacteristically deep sleep. When I awoke I found myself locked in a room the size of a walk-in closet, while the temperature steadily fell until it was below freezing. They wanted to see how well Ankylos tolerate harsh climates as a test of our survival. It's known that Drakon can withstand weather extremes quite well. But they were unsure about hybrids.

It turns out that us Ankylos tolerate extreme weather better than humans but worse than our fullblood ancestors. And, extreme cold temperatures negatively affect Ankylos faster than extreme heat. The warden and his guards found this out by subjecting some Ankylos prisoners to a heat room that gradually became hotter, while locking me inside the Ice Room.

I didn't last as long as those in the heat room and eventually passed out from the cold. Upon being revived, the warden informed me that I would likely have fallen into cardiac arrest if I'd stayed in there for five minutes longer. Still, this experiment went on twice more, even after he knew my limit, which made me realize he just got off on having someone much stronger than him at his complete mercy. He reveled in the power of controlling a person's fate, holding their life in his grasp. And when they teetered on the brink of death, knowing he alone could decide to either bring them back from the precipice or let them slip into a cold, eternal slumber. A true monster.

Admittedly, there's one last thing I won't admit to him. He's changed me physically. The stressful conditions and constant threat of death seemed to have awoken what I can only guess is my dormant Drakon DNA. It's like my body has become stronger as a defense mechanism to keep me alive. The same fist that could always crack another man's bone can now dent the concrete and bend the metal bed frame anchored to the wall. I've been testing my newly increased strength against the bars themselves, and they've started to groan.

My senses have sharpened as well. I see better in the dark. I hear conversations behind closed doors, and smells can overwhelm me. Lately, I've noticed how my body tingles at the sweet, red currant scent lingering in my space. It's cool and honeyed, with hints of cream and fresh oranges. So goddamn enticing and feminine it takes my breath away.

I force it all away before my body betrays me. It reacts to that scent without my will. Without my goddamn permission. And of all the indecencies I've endured, a hard-on in Goldilocks' face isn't one I'll accept.

Every day, he visits, watching me as if waiting for something more. No matter how hard I contemplate it, I cannot decide his goal. Does he simply want to learn more about Ankylos physiology, or is he looking to create Ankylos slaves? Maybe he just wants to watch us slowly die. What does he gain from these experiments?

"You can tell me the truth, you know," says the warden, trying to sound humane. "I just want to ensure you're feeling alright after your last incident. Despite what you may think, I care about my inmates."

Incident, he says, like these slashes on my chest and back just *happened* to me. Like he didn't *choose* to have me stripped, chained, and whipped bloody while the guards laughed. The freshly regenerated scales over my shoulder blades still itch.

I may have killed an elected official, but that bastard deserved it. All corrupt politicians do. He headed the trafficking of Ankylos children into an underground parlor to be abused by his equally corrupt friends. When they were discovered, all his associates were charged, yet somehow, the owner of this parlor was found "not guilty." Somehow, he was allowed to continue running his municipality as if nothing happened because, I guess, hybrid children don't matter enough to the country for a charismatic official to lose his job.

Honestly, I'd kill him again if I could.

Anyway, offing him was worth it. It landed me here, exactly where I need to be to protect my people. Based on my own *punishments*, I know they keep the isolation cells and torture rooms underground, and they're always full of hybrids. I don't know how many or what state they're in.

There's a headache building behind my eyes as I imagine the day I get free of this place. How I'll task Knox with gathering the addresses of every single guard that's had a hand in the tortures. He'll send an enforcer to every door and make sure my point is understood. If he doesn't die during my jailbreak, I'll save the warden for last, visit him quietly, alone, and repay him for everything he's graciously shown me.

"Alright, Kalen," he murmurs, almost apologetically, though I know better. "I guess if you won't give me answers, your body will have to."

The sound of metal grinding follows his words, revealing another prisoner being held by a guard. He's a Veloc, a skilled hunting species of alien hybrid that does exceptionally well with tracking targets for The Divide. I don't know him. Never seen him before, but in our shared situation, I empathize with him.

Neither of us wants to be here, and only one of us can leave. I spare him a glance because I feel a duty to remember the faces of the ones I kill.

There's nothing I can do to stop what happens next. If there's one thing I've learned, it's that *Goldilocks* won't let either of us out until one of us is dead.

So I crack my neck as they release his wrists and hand him a crude shank.

Inhale. Exhale.

I blink, and then he's on me.

Chapter 2 - Mel

There is nothing glamorous about being in prison.

Not the cinder block walls nor the view of the cracked asphalt parking lot. Not the miserable toilets or the sweltering heat. Certainly not the *two hots and a cot* where the food isn't fit for a dog, and the beds feel worse than sleeping on the floor.

Other housing facilities might be better, but ProMaxim, short for *Prolonged Maximum Security*, isn't one of the good ones. As the most impenetrable criminal housing facility in the tri-regional area, it imprisons the worst of the worst, anyone from hybrid hitmen to human serial killers—monsters of every kind, shape, and form.

It's the kiss of death for many. And, assuming it was designed to parallel how the hardened criminals behind its bars treated their victims, I might not mind the facilities if I didn't have to be here too.

I desperately want to scratch at the cheap tag irritating the back of my neck. I scrunch the sleeves on this oversized uniform, hoping to at least catch a hint of a breeze. Lately, I've been soaking the material through, and judging by my guard, Chaz, I seem to be the only one sweating half to death.

Thank goodness I did a big chop last month, and now I'm rocking a short-cropped style because if I had my bra-strap-length curls to deal with, I'd probably overheat.

A loud beep echoes beside me, followed by the grating sound of a heavy metal door sliding open. I used to startle when a cell opened, much to the amusement of the guards. Now, I only wince, thoroughly adjusted to my new reality.

My future therapy bill is climbing by the minute.

"Ugh, Chaz, that's *foul*. What did you have for lunch, chili?" I grumble, retching behind a hand.

"Don't even start, Mel," he sighs, not taking me seriously because we both know exactly where the odor is coming from.

Chaz steps back without a word, lingering humor in the air as he resumes his position in the hallway. Of all the prison guards here, I like him the best because he doesn't pry or flirt. He doesn't ignore me when I try to make conversation or stare at my ass when I bend over. I'm so comfortable with Chaz that I don't bother glancing over my shoulder as I enter the cell, carting as many supplies as possible.

The same hands that once fed the most ruthless man in the city now cramps around a cleaning basket. The thought makes me pause. *Why is that the first accolade that comes to mind?* I've accomplished a lot on my own, *always on my own.* So, why would my servitude be what defines me? I make it two more steps into the cell before I have to stop from the smell alone. *God, it's awful.* I manage another sip of air through my mouth and hold it.

I'll work on some practiced mindfulness when I get home. *I am not my struggles. My trauma does not define me.* Nodding with the redirection, I take in the scene.

There's blood on the floor, arching up two walls and splattering the ceiling. There's a rusty lump of metal, plastic, and wood on the concrete floor and the most heinous pool of blood trailing toward the drain. It looks like soup now, thick and congealed as it dries.

Nobody gets paid enough for this. Mentally, I hear my therapy bill *cha-ching* again.

As depressing as my life was for the months leading up to now — when I feared an overcooked steak might mean a brutal fist to the head — this death trap has managed to make me miss it. I don't miss Drew. In fact, my father better hope I never catch him crawling out of whatever hole he's hiding in.

But I do miss the joy of painting my restaurant storefront. Printing the first menus. Flipping the *open* sign every morning. The blind optimism that whispered *finally.*

I miss the days when all my dreams were coming true, one perfect plate at a time. The restaurant wasn't fit for royalty, but it was affordable, easily some of the best cuisine in New Almos, and it was *mine.*

Or so I thought.

Turns out my father took out the loan of a lifetime against my budding business—my baby. How does a man with two bankruptcies and no job borrow half a million dollars?

Not from a bank, I can promise you that much. Not from any human establishment at all, actually.

He sold my business to criminals as collateral—monstrous ones at that. The Divide. For all intents and purposes, he sold *me.* And my *potential - th*e potential profit margins of my restaurant, the potential benefit of a chef under their thumb. And maybe there's another reason I'm missing as well. Was I also sold to be some potential mate to a Divide member?

It's that last one that marks his damn days as numbered. I could forgive Drew for the rest. Hell, he's only a creature of habit, and I knew better than to let him back into my life after my child-hood. But the thought of being sold as property? As something to be claimed and mated as they wish?

Yeah, there's a filet knife I've been sharpening at home with my father's name on it.

Apparently, bloodlines mattered more to monsters than sense, the name on the rental agreement, and the goddamn truth.

Or so it seemed to The Divide and Crowe, their leader. My body trembles at the thought of him, his muscular build and towering presence that dominates every room he enters. His skin is a unique shade of deep gray, perfectly contrasting his mesmerizing jade-green eyes.

I can't lie — seeing a man *that* dominating and handsome sitting in my dark apartment with that look in his eyes did something to me. If he were any other kind of male, I would probably be dead because instead of screaming when I had the chance, *before* someone could throw a rough palm over my mouth, I simply *sighed*. Sighed! Like he was a dream made real. Like he was here to secretly bring a fantasy to life.

Lord, I never said I was your strongest soldier. It's been a *while* since I've been on any type of ride. Sue me.

The Divide is the criminal organization everyone in New Almos knows not to cross. It acts as a parent company with tentacles all over the city. It's involved in everything from money laundering and illegal casinos to assassinations, loan sharking, security, and other seedy services. Or so I've heard. The latter is likely what motivates the Prime Minister to keep them around even though nearly everything they do is highly illegal. Hell, maybe he keeps them around for everything.

I only made it two months before my father's mistakes caught up with me. Two months before, I became Crowe's personal chef and his glorified servant.

I even miss that, not for Crowe, but for the food. The fancy dinners he hosted for the elite. Laidback spreads as thank-yous to his enforcers. Simple desserts. Beautiful place settings. Creative freedom. It went on like that for months, a delicate rhythm where he demanded to be fed, and I obliged.

Then he murdered a New Almos municipality government official, and everything changed.

When he was found guilty and sentenced to this hell hole overnight, the boss of The Divide *should've* taken my debt with him. I *should've* been free to return to my restaurant and my life. I suppose I did ultimately get that. I just got this task, too, because freedom isn't free.

And based on the horror I've been cleaning on my knees for the past month, I might not be free anytime soon.

Leaning closer, I stop near the severed tip of an ear on the floor. I can't whistle worth a damn, but it shocks the sound out of me.

"You have to use your tongue," Chaz sighs from the hall. "It sounds like you're passing gas."

"First of all, no, it doesn't," I defend, crouching down to inspect the floor splatter. I gag this time, throat thickening over the putrid scent. How long did this sit here before they called? Why didn't the day shift clean it?

My shoulders are already aching in anticipation of removing dried blood from every surface. I toss over my left shoulder,

"And when I do the tongue thing, I sound like that cartoon duck. You know, the one that spits."

He laughs, the sound harsh and far too loud in the silence of the halls. They've cleared the whole cell block for my safety, yet I always feel like I'm being watched. Sweat runs down the bridge of my nose until my forearm swipes it away.

"Try it, lemme see if you're right."

"*Ass*," I mutter. "I'm not giving you any more ammo. I still haven't lived down the break room incident."

"You mean that f—"

"IT WAS THE CHAIR! How many times do I have to tell you that when you sit down on plastic too fast, it— you know what? Go to hell. You know exactly what happened." My neck is hot, the heat creeping up my chin and cheeks until the sweat that beads across my forehead is worse than before.

Maybe I'm coming down with something, and this is a fever.

"Yeah, I put the pieces together," he says with another laugh. "Just let whistling go. It's not your calling."

It's not your calling, I mock silently with a flick of my head.

"Saw that."

"Why don't you *see* some damn halls to keep me safe instead of worrying about whether I can or can *not* whistle."

"You can't, though." There's a huff, then more silence. It forces me back to the task and how much I'd rather be laid on my bed, eating a fresh batch of sugar cookies. Maybe I'll bake instead of trying to get a restless few hours of sleep after my shift. I swallow the lump that forms in my throat after the next inhale. Suddenly, all I taste is bile and the tang of rancid blood in the air. Maybe eating is off the table for a while.

Thankfully, the dead body is gone; that's not always the case here. I'm not even sure how prisoners get inside these cells. ProMaxim houses every inmate in isolation except for meal times and an hour of mobility. Though the number of bloody crime scenes I've cleaned up over the last month makes me think there's some intention behind the attacks.

If I can find out exactly how inmates are getting around their restrictions, I might be able to use that to my advantage.

I glance around the space, even though I know exactly whose cell I'm standing in. It seems strange that a man who killed a government official has been given amenities I've seen nowhere else. None of the other cells have a desk, a window that isn't completely obscured, or a mini fridge. They don't have several uniformed jumpsuits hanging on a metal bar near their bed.

How does he have so much power here?

I've cleaned his cell almost weekly, and the prison guards are either trying their hardest to kill him or simply leading lambs to their slaughter. Based on his amenities, I'm betting it's the latter.

I wonder if the warden knows.

They've got someone to do their dirty work, and Crowe's morals are low enough not to care.

That isn't entirely true. My mind unhelpfully supplied moments when I'd respected him, even if they were only stolen from between the cracked kitchen door.

I recall his eyes from one of the only times I ever saw him lose his temper. They were bright, almost glowing, when he turned to face the alien hybrid on his knees. He was kneeling in a pool of his own piss, paper-thin wings shaking behind him. I had thought they were beautiful until I saw the kind of man they were attached to. Crowe did not care about the man's fear, the jade of his eyes eating away at whatever emotions were underneath. But the Ptero deserved it. Hitting women, whether alien or human, was prohibited within The Divide. Aside from interrogation tactics used during capture, apparently, women were never harmed.

The beating that followed had been more than justified, and those wings had looked just as beautiful in pieces on the floor.

As irritating as it is, I'm clear proof of Crowe's morals, too. Sure, I may hate my situation with a passion, but even I can see how much worse it could have been. My eyes dart to the blood-coated book in his room. Even though I know it'll be empty, just like the last three times, I make a mental note to check.

"Was a pretty bad fight," Chaz murmurs from beyond the metal doorway, cutting off the thought and confirming what I've already deduced. The interruption draws my eyes from the book. "You've got an hour before we need to leave."

An hour.

To clean up all this blood? I breathe in the metallic, musty scent of old blood once more and fight the water stinging in my eyes. It isn't going anywhere until I clean it up. So I pull my goggles over my eyes, tug up the face mask dangling at my neck, and spray down as much of the blood as I can, watching it flow down the drain. Then I pour hydrogen peroxide on the bloodstains left behind.

Briefly, it occurs to me that all my biggest problems in life revolved around or were caused by men. I curse them all under my breath.

Fuck Drew. Fuck Crowe and Knox. Fuck The Divide.

Chapter 3 - Mel

I can't help but try to visualize the scene while the peroxide soaks—where the men stood, how the weapon drew all this blood, and how long it took the liquid to leave the body. It's strangely enticing to think of Crowe in this visceral way. What kind of alien is he? From what I remember, his features align closely with the Ankylos I've seen around the penthouse, but he doesn't have the scales, and his horns aren't as long, either.

I watch the peroxide start to foam, lifting the bloodstains from the floor. I know my way around a knife, but this is different. Brutal, raw. Desperate. It's like the body was hacked apart.

As I wipe away the foam and begin to treat the surface of the floor with an enzymatic stain remover, I can't help but wonder what Crowe must look like unleashed.

Girl, what?

I pause, mortified at my intrusive thoughts. I have officially lost my mind if I'm thinking about my boss like that. Yeah, in the dark kitchen, I might have admired his appearance, but now that I'm in this situation, I don't even consider it. If I thought glimpses of what The Divide enforcers can do scared me, seeing evidence of Crowe's brutality rearranges my mind. That's what I blame my momentary insanity on. Oh, and a crazy obsession with dangerous men I can't have.

The way I build him up probably isn't even real. Or healthy. He's too strong and dominating. He's too patient and controlled. Too generous yet punishing at the same time. I sigh aloud. Men are always more disappointing if you build them up in your head first because no one is perfect. *Technically, he's not entirely a man, though, is he? Non-human blood runs through his veins.* My mind annoys me with distracting observations I don't ask for. I'm avoiding those thoughts for a reason, but then there's my brain, not giving a single crap.

A lot of humans see hybrids as monsters, as inherently dangerous, and standing in a cell filled with the blood of what used to be another living being, I can understand it. That's not to say I think it's right that many of their population are ostracized in this country due to the violent tendencies of some. Humans have our own brand of violent and fucked up — arguably worse than any other species.

Due to decades of mixing with humans, many hybrids that you encounter on a daily basis are almost indistinguishable from us, that is, until you look closer and spot things that are slightly off, like eye color, elongated fingers with clawed tips, fangs...

I've noticed that The Divide seems to attract the rest: the hybrids who possess physical traits that immediately stand out and are harder to conceal, like wings, spikes, height, build, tails, horns, and the like. Perhaps it's because their differences awaken an instinctual unease amongst humans. Their unique and startling features remind us, humans, just how fragile we are without our war machines and guns. How easy it would be for aliens to rule over us or take us out if they wanted to.

It crosses my mind that I probably wouldn't mind an alien takeover if it meant my loans would disappear. But, I don't think that's their goal. Human and hybrid relations have been tense, especially in parts of the world like this one. Relations improved a lot over the past decades, but hybrids still find themselves fighting to be seen as regular citizens. To carve out their own place in society and be wholly accepted.

I admire their resilience. I see it in them every day. It suddenly dawns on me that some Divide members probably sought refuge in that organization for companionship, and perhaps others simply couldn't find regular work and turned to one of the only companies that would hire them.

Not everything is black and white, I remind myself.

My mind wanders back to Crowe and how he could have easily held a decent job in human society. His features, though foreign or what some would call 'exotic,' are not unpleasant, and he has the height and build that many men respect. He could have become a CEO somewhere, maybe a government official under the Prime Minister. But instead, he built The Divide up with his bare hands—or so I've heard, one body at a time. I can imagine it now in a way that never fully sank in before. I'm afraid of that kind of raw power, but it isn't *fear* that makes my pulse pound and sweat slide between my breasts.

And I refuse to consider it.

"Come on, Melanie, get to work. You don't want Crowe returning from the infirmary to see you in his room, and the rest of the cell block will finish the second meal soon. I don't know about you, but I'd rather not guard against an entire sector."

I shiver. However, it's the thought of which guards might be escorting him that gets me moving. They're the ones I truly have to watch. After all, how does a prisoner get into a locked cell?

He's *let* in.

I shiver again. Can I use the same tactics to let someone *out*?

An unsettling memory from last night enters my mind. I'm at home when Knox pays me a visit. I let him in. I have no choice. He strolls past me and heads for the kitchen. I follow him, and it's there that he gives me a most ridiculous and dangerous mission. I instantly refuse it. But I quickly learn I never had a choice as he grabs me by the throat.

"It has to be you, Melanie," Knox grits out between squeezes of my neck. It's the look on his face that stills my fighting reflexes. His

eyes are wild with worry, his fangs bared. "They have a record of every member. Every girlfriend. Every business partner!"

"There has to be someone else! I'm a chef! Not ... whatever this is. I don't - I'm not a criminal, Knox. I don't know what I'm doing. I haven't found anything for weeks. And he's never in his cell when I'm there."

"Then you'd better learn. And fast. My brother owns you. You like that restaurant? That dream? Your goddamn life? Then you'll do whatever you're told."

This sonofabitch. "There's only so much I can do without any leads. Maybe you could hire — "

" — You're the only one the feds don't care about. They don't know what you look like or care who cooked my brother's steaks. We can't get words inside. We can't get eyes inside. It has to be you, end of discussion!" He punctuates his point with a knock of my head against the wall, tightening his grip over my throat before shoving me away.

I hate that my limbs are frozen, and I'm genuinely shaken up. Emotions make people unpredictable, and with Knox especially, I'm not sure how close I am to real harm. Shaking with unshed tears behind my eyes, I slump against my kitchen wall, wondering if I'll ever feel safe again. Wondering if I'll ever be free.

I shake the memory and blink away tears that pool in my eyes. I won't cry here. I can't. Instead, I study the hydrogen peroxide-soaked stains, absently touching the fresh bruise beneath my uniform. Reaching up, I unzip it a little to allow for more air. My throat is tight, and the room's heat is oppressive.

Knox, Crowe's brother, is many things, and based on my home visit last night, patient isn't one of them. But I can't give him answers that I don't have. I can't find quick solutions to problems I've never solved before. And, frankly, that I never created.

With a grimace, I begin scrubbing death's residue away, cursing my luck with every sloppy glide of my brush. The cramp in my shoulder blade is nothing compared to the pain in my throat. My neck is hot and irritated, reminding me just how sore it is with each swallow.

I've managed to make it through most of the room regardless of the pain, strategically stopping near the bookshelf where my target lies. As I get closer, I recognize the book, its title written in a foreign language. Not for the first time, I ponder just how many languages Crowe can understand.

I swipe and spray at the blood trail as I head for it, hoping Chaz is occupied with guard duty. His radio buzzed a few minutes ago, and he walked away, talking to someone on the other end. I glance over my shoulder to see he still hasn't returned.

The book in my hands is a tattered, mass-produced lump of pages barely held together by tape over the spine, and yet, judging by the age, it's important to Crowe. Something he managed to smuggle into jail with him. The cost to keep it is probably high, so despite how I feel about the man, I'm careful. After gently peeling back the cover, I check the third page where I left my original note.

Sure, it was risky to attempt covert communication. We could be caught, and if Knox was right about me being the only one who could pull this off, such a mistake could cost me everything. It was even riskier tucking the note into a book I wasn't sure Crowe read regularly, if at all.

It's a testament to how unfit for this job I am. I don't know the first thing about criminals or how to gain information from strangers. I don't know how to be sneaky or manipulative. But then, I see a tiny scrap of paper near the spine, folded so tightly, it looks like a wad of trash.

The first pulse of victory goes through my chest.

Success, my heart screams, though I won't know to what degree until I get back to the break room. It's liable to say nothing. Or tell me to figure it the fuck out. It might even be actual trash.

Still, before Chaz returns, I slip the wad into my pocket and wipe the cover clean. There's an electronic beep followed by the rough grating sound of the cell door moving.

My shoulder stings and my throat burns, but when I turn around, neither matters, because Crowe is standing in the doorway to his cell, and the metal bars are sliding closed.

Chapter 4 - Mel

This place has changed him. Or am I remembering him wrong?

Except for those striking green eyes and his height, I hardly recognize him at all. His hair has grown out and falls a few inches past his shoulders in brown waves. His jumpsuit has been half removed and tied around his waist, making it apparent that the skin around his throat and shoulders is a canvas of scales that shimmer like the midnight sea. They're also a shade or two darker than the rest of him. His horns look longer than I remember. They appear to have a spiral-like pattern to them as well. I've never noticed that before. Or how sharp and pronounced his jawline is.

Teeth don't just keep growing into maturity, human or otherwise. I know this, and yet, his fangs are definitely longer and more predatory. Even the way he cocks his head to the side is unfamiliar. As if he's figuring out whether to attack me.

His shoulders and arms look larger than they once had in his suits. Perhaps he's been working out here, which is not uncommon in prison, a place with very little to do.

I've never been alone with Crowe long enough to notice any of those more intimate details, like the shape of his clawed hands, the spread of thick thighs in the unflattering uniform. I notice all these details about him now and file them away in my mind. After all, I'm not above admiring an attractive male.

The silence in the room is so loud it reminds me that we're alone. *Alone.*

When I worked as his chef, there was always staff moving around between the rooms anytime that I prepared food during the days. In the evenings, there were always guards and enforcers or foot soldiers. We were *never* alone. It's shocking how quickly my body loses grip on reality when facing his presence without a buffer.

He's tall.

The distance between us is the only reason I don't have to crane my neck.

With arms like that, he could probably pick me up and throw me over his shoulder.

My eyes widen in shock. Where are all these thoughts coming from? It's one thing to idly find Crowe attractive while I'm serving him dinner, the twist of my stomach now is an entirely different thing. Especially with us imprisoned in a bloody cell.

My legs start shaking first, and the next breath is hollow, catching in my throat until it burns right where the bruise sits. It's the fever. It has to be some sort of brain delirium.

He studies my face intensely, cocking his head the other way to get a different angle. Does he not recognize me? Being forgettable comes with an unexpected sting, one that reminds me of my relationship with my father, Drew. How he'd disappear without warning for years at a time. How his abandonment would always leave me feeling disorientated. Undervalued. *Wounded*.

I shove those thoughts of my father away, hearing my therapy bill rise again.

If Crowe notices my inner turmoil, he doesn't show it. Gone are the tailored suits over broad shoulders and cigars, the hostile civility and wealth. Gone are the flashy women and fast cars, the dinner parties, and shows of force. There was always so much distance between that leader and the rest of the world. But what remains, what's standing in front of me, is the person beneath it all.

His dark brows are deeply furrowed, shadowing eyes that look a little unfocused. His wavy hair is pulled into a half bun, the rest hanging over his shoulders. The dark strands only serve to highlight his complexion. Was he always this pale? He almost looks sick.

My thoughts are consumed by the image of his rich, slate-gray skin, against the crisp white collar of his dress shirts, and his sable brown hair slicked away from his eyes to curl at his neck. His skin glistens with sweat, and his breaths are heavy and uneven. His cheeks are tinged with a maroon hue, giving him the appearance of a person who had just emerged from a wild run.

What the hell is going on here?

I have the laughable urge to cool his clammy skin with a wet towel. Or prepare a pot of *Gohdawb* stew. It's an herbal broth with goat, vegetables, and rice. A traditional meal among the Ankylos youth who are just growing their horns and scales. Apparently, it helps with regeneration and pain. I just think it tastes delicious, which is why I learned how to make it in the first place.

He looks like he needs it now. *Damn*, I could probably cut carrots on his jawline. His bone structure makes him look a little more severe, as if his stature weren't imposing enough. His cheekbones are still defined, hollowing his face. Crowe looks tired, exhausted, actually. And there's a bruise blooming over his temple.

His mouth opens around what looks like my name, but he snaps it closed instead, his eyes jerking around the room like someone else will appear. Were his teeth sharper than normal? For that brief moment, they looked like blades.

Now isn't the time for ridiculous fears when there is enough to be afraid of already. I flick my eyes over his broad shoulders to see my idiotic guard, but there's no one. To my dismay, Chaz hasn't appeared, so it's only us.

Crowe swallows, running his eyes over me like there is a concealed weapon under my uniform. His eyes fix on my neck, and his gaze sharpens. My heart pounds under the weight of his stare.

I lower my gaze, suddenly nervous for some inexplicable reason. My eyes sweep over his naked torso and the densely packed muscle beneath his lean stomach, but they quickly snap up to his chest, lingering on the raw skin there. He sees me notice the irritated skin, and his fist curls. Only the right fist because the left is in a sling. With three fingers on his hand wrapped in white medical tape.

Then I realize that his brow has stabilizing tape holding the skin together, and his lower lip is busted, swollen slightly. He would be pouting if it wasn't for the fire in his glittering eyes, daring me to ... I'm not sure.

On his elongated, pointed ears, he wears small, gold hooped earrings. He always has, as far as I remember, but presently, the tip of his right ear is torn. I swear I don't mean to notice these details, but I almost can't help it. I look up, risking a quick glance at his face. He's already staring at me, and our eyes meet once more. A flurry of emotions rushes through me: feelings of pity, fear, and something else. Something primal and forbidden.

The sound he makes — it causes me to jerk backward, hitting the wall and smearing my shoulder against the still-wet bloodstains.

I've never heard anyone growl like that before, and I'm not sure how to react to the prickle of desire it stirs within my body. Once again, my eyes are drawn to his bare chest, but this time, I noticed his nipples. They're erect just as mine are, though this uniform thankfully conceals them.

As I blink and try to process my emotions, his chest seems to expand. But it's not really growing; it's just getting closer and closer. I inhale sharply as another wave of desire washes over me, an unwelcome but undeniable sensation heightened by the warmth emanating from his body.

My gaze goes to my shaking hands keeping me upright on the wall, then to the cleaning supplies, and back to the man scowling down at me. As if my body can't help it, my back bows slightly, pressing my chest toward him. This is wrong on many levels. It's not the right time or place. Hell, it certainly isn't even the right person! This is the man I work for. And not only is he currently a prisoner, but even if circumstances were different, there's no guarantee he even desires humans.

While some hybrids are open to relationships with humans, many prefer to find companionship amongst each other. And I get it. Humans are like this, too, often gravitating toward those who share our race, ethnicity, or national background. We're creatures of habit, instinctively seeking out the comfort of the familiar. Until recently, I thought I fell into this category, too. But clearly, it's become evident that my preferences are far more expansive than I had initially realized. Maybe he feels similarly if the tension between us is anything to go by.

I'm suddenly aware of just how hot it is as a bead of sweat drips down the back of my neck. This close, I realize he smells earthy and masculine, like vetiver mixed with bergamot. Addictive, and pleasant enough that I no longer smell the gore. It's distracting. And, strangely enough, soothing.

His scowl stops me from leaning forward to inhale again. He's angry about something.

Maybe he expected me to figure out a plan much faster than this. I hadn't considered how bad the last month might have been for him. It's not my job to consider Crowe's feelings, but the panic growing in my chest worsens because maybe he's been fighting for his life while I moan about the hardship of cleaning dirty floors.

Shame is a strange thing to feel when I'm fully justified in hating my boss. I'm *owed* my hatred, at the very least. And still, I'm a bit ashamed that I haven't tried harder to do my job. The job he doesn't seem to understand as he eyes my supplies with suspicion. Then, Crowe steals a quick glance at the book behind me, the one still askew from when I was startled. Something must have finally registered to him because he's studying me even more intently, working something out in his mind.

Again, I remember that I'm forgettable. Background noise. I ignore the ache in my throat.

Knox said they couldn't get a man on the inside. He swore they couldn't get word in or out, couldn't get eyes on his brother at all. Suddenly, I understood his panic when he pinned me to my front door. My hand finds its way to my throat as I realize something else.

Crowe has no idea why I'm here. Or what I've been asked to do. Did he think I had come here to harm him?

When I take the first step toward the cell door, I find his eyes on my throat again. Absently, I drop my hand away and slowly gesture toward my supplies. I'm worried that a single word may trigger him.

He blocks the way with two quick steps. "Why are you here?"

"I'm just doing my job," I say evenly, forcing myself to sound calmer than I feel. "Cleaning." I'm hoping he can read between the lines in the way I emphasize the words, but I can't be sure. Not until he steps back with a dismissive rough sound, rounding my shaking form toward the back wall.

The way he growls almost pulls the truth from me. It's not from his throat, but rather from within his chest, predatory and loud, and *dammit*, the sound goes straight between my legs. This is inappropriate. Illogical. Reckless. I'm not even sure what I feel, why my pulse is racing, nor why the idea of his body caging me in makes me dizzy.

This is my boss. A criminal. The monster who holds the keys to my freedom and the man who makes me want things I can't have.

Turning to follow his slow retreat, I realize his bed sheets are stained with blood splatter. I take a deep breath before speaking. "There's extra sheets in the hall," I manage, taking another careful step toward the exit.

He remains silent, just nods curtly, and keeps his eyes glued to me as if I might explode and kill us both.

The weight of his stare is addictive. I don't think he's ever so much as glanced at me since I first arrived here and now he won't look away. He lifts one thick thigh to lean onto the desk. It's barely sitting and hardly standing, making me wonder if he has more bruises than I can see. It would make sense for how tightly he's holding himself, every muscle straining in his arms as he crosses them.

"Melanie!" A voice yells, shattering the moment. It's Chaz yelling from beyond the bars. Three other guards round the cell beside him, their guns drawn on the quiet prisoner. Something about it strikes me as odd, but I can't figure out what.

"Mel, I'm so sorry. The warden called ... never mind, it doesn't matter. *Prisoner 1838, Kalen Crowe,* I will be opening this cell door. If you so much as twitch, you will be tranqed and rendered unconscious. If you attempt to attack any of us, including your cleaner, you will be placed in isolation for a length of time to be determined by the warden. Do you understand?"

Kalen.

I've never known his first name, but it suits him. Not that it matters what I think. Not that I should be thinking about anything except escaping the confines of this cell. He remains silent, looking visibly upset, his body tense as he leans against his desk.

Then Chaz's words fully register in my mind. So they're willing to send him to isolation if he attacks me, but when he butchers another inmate, he gets nothing?

My inner voice is screaming how odd that is. I want to consider it further, but the anger rolling off of him is blanketing the room in more heat than I know what to do with. My eyes close, dizzying as my body sways before I catch myself near the bars.

"She hasn't finished," his voice comes from behind me, so close I can feel his warm breath brush the back of my neck. Surprisingly, no one in the hall shouts at him for approaching me. No one raises a gun.

"She stays until it's clean," Kalen Crowe says. And to my horror, no one disagrees.

Chapter 5 - Kalen

S omething is dripping down my back. Searing. Too warm. It's all too warm. Another whistle of wind slices the room before the leather splits my skin. I welcome the burning because, at least then, I cannot daydream of sinking into her heat. She's following me, invading my mind no matter the circumstances.

I don't understand it.

In this cell, there is only me and this punishment. The warden near the exit. The man holding the whip. These cold, hard chains holding me to my knees. Everything else is obscured in shadows. The light from one of their pocket beams only illuminates enough for them to see each strike land.

And land, they do. Again. And again.

All because I'm denying the warden something he wants. *What is it?* I can't seem to remember.

I am not entirely alone; the doe-eyed cleaner is also in the room with me. Not physically, but as an intrusive vision floods my mind. I can see her leaning towards me, her tongue darting out to lick the blood drying on my neck. I imagine her moaning for me as if she did not know her mate's blood would be sweet. My cock throbs until I shove the illusion aside, choosing instead to concentrate on the pain that spreads across my restrained body.

I *can't* think of her here. Not now when *he* might see too much and recognize my weaknesses.

The whip sings again, and my back bows.

I think the scent of her lingered in my cell for hours. I think it has been lingering for days. Maybe weeks. But not this severely. Has it been sinking under my skin this whole time? Her scent in my cell was a problem. Her standing there in the flesh was my undoing.

And all that's left is this ache.

She's so intoxicating I couldn't help but demand she stay and finish the job. Drops of sweat glided down her throat as she worked, scrubbing the horror of my latest test away. I wanted to taste those streaks marking her skin. Were they sweet? Salty? Warm or cool? The savagery of my urge was shocking, leaving me stunned in silence; the only sound was the swish of the brush.

Something hard slams into my jaw, rocking the world off-kilter. The memory dissolves and reshapes.

There was a guard staring at her on her hands and knees. I remember that now. She was there for me, but he was watching her. Watching as her back moved with each stroke of the brush. I switched my focus to him instead, my heart beating with an anger I could barely contain nor understand. Why did his presence suddenly irritate me? I had little time to mull over this as the sight of the beautiful, brown-skinned woman leaving the cell and returning to the other side of the bars sent me crashing back to reality. A reality void of the admiring friends and colleagues I was used to. Void of the talented chef-turned-cleaner who had just left.

She belongs here with me, the most primal part of my mind declares. *No.* She doesn't belong anywhere *near* here. But she does belong with *me*. Always with me.

A blend of red-currant and cream and fresh oranges. So sweet and refreshing. So familiar, it burned from my chest to my gut as I watched her walk past the leering guard. The other one, Chaz, I think is his name, had checked her over frantically. He will be allowed to live. But the one whose eyes can't stop wandering is a different story.

He stared long after she was gone like she wasn't *mine*. Like he didn't know what I would do to him the second my cell door opened.

My nail beds itched as my claws emerged. I took a single swing at the guard who had been leering at my chef-turned-cleaner, and his jaw bone shattered like glass, or the brittle currant hard candies from my youth. He screamed bloody murder and fell to his knees, scrambling away from me. I turned to see Chaz backing away from me as well, his hands up, terror evident in his eyes. He was telling me to "calm down and return to my cell" and that "I really didn't want to do this." Oh, but I did.

And I had for a while now.

The leering guard with the broken jaw had suddenly found strength enough to rise to his feet, turn, and run down the nearby mobility tunnel. I gave chase, catching up to him quickly, and grabbed the back of his shirt.

My teeth met the flesh of his throat and tore. When had my fangs become so sharp? When had I decided to *bite*? I don't recall ever having this urge when angered in the past. I only recall how the guard bled everywhere as I gave chase. He was gasping and choking on words that didn't matter. Would never matter. Because she was mine. Not his. Not any of theirs.

The mobility tunnel usually smells like sanitizer mixed with sweat. But I made it smell like blood. The first splatter wasn't enough. Not even when he screamed and begged. Not even when the blood wet the concrete...

I'm brought back to the present when I feel something like a boot press deeply, painfully into the back of my knee until I fear it will break. My pained moans turn into full-on screams that I'd never want her to hear.

It's better that she's not really here.

Red currant and cream. Oranges. Her scent is suffocating me slowly. Thankfully, it's everywhere. In the air, under my nails. I think it's in my nose as they break me down into pieces. This punishment is because they found the guard. And I do not care. I'm beyond such things when I'm drowning in her. It soothes the parts of me that hurt: my back, my legs, and my shoulders. The warden walks through her specter and looks pleased. He even smiles at the thing I'm becoming.

At whatever tears from my shoulder blades and spine.

It shoots out of me so quickly I fall. I'm falling toward her. She's on her knees, the sight erotic and damning. She's in my head. The cleaner. What's her name? The guard said it, but it's gone now. My mind didn't hold it. How could I ever forget her face?

She's mine.

The chains snap against my wrists, holding me steady to stop my fall. My head slumps. Where is she? Where is she? Where? Two guards unshackle my body and re-latch me to the bed, my arms straining tight against new wall restraints.

Whatever happened to my back, I feel stuck to the bed, unable to turn or stand. My shoulders are screaming so severely I can no longer feel the pain in my knee or my back. Though the blood still drips. Still soaks through the mattress and flimsy blanket. I hear it dripping to the floor.

I'm alone after that. Prone and vulnerable — my arms bound tight while I bleed and drown in her essence. She's under my skin, burrowed between my ribs. Achingly soft. It seems insane that a body can die from *want* before it dies from blood loss. And to add insult to injury, I'm so goddamn hard that every ounce of blood has fled my brain, damn the leaking wounds. Damn, what I need to survive.

I only need to cum. If I could just mark her with it. If she were only willing to -

I'm nothing but flesh and need, and it's taking everything not to think of my cock. Not to beg for the pressure to be released.

It's angry. I'm angry. We're both frustrated and *starved* for red currant and cream. For oranges. For the tangy warmth and sweetness on my tongue. If I could just relieve the pressure...

I can't reach into the torn jumpsuit anyway with my arms hanging from above. My shoulder joints grind as they stretch. But even the pain can't kill it, the erection as aggressive as its owner. It's as aggressive as her hold over me.

Who is she? Who?

There's pressure behind my eyes, and her ghostly figure emerges in front of me. It's far too dark to see anything at all. I'm imagining it, seeing her as I close my eyes, and it will have to be enough because—

Melanie Williams.

Her name pierces through the fog in my mind. I can finally attach a name to the face that has been haunting me. My chef.

My restauranteur. Drew's foolish daughter. It's all a bit jumbled in my head.

Before, I never felt ... Her scent was never this ...

I hardly recognize the way she appears through these new eyes.

But she's perfect in every way.

She's hovering in my peripheral now, whispering too softly. I cannot hear her over the ringing in my ears. She rounds my shoulder, returning from a view of my back, her eyes sad and teary. Too brown. Too soft. Almost like the night, I came to collect her father's debt.

Her apartment was small, nestled onto a quiet block in the underdeveloped side of town. The locks were brittle, far too easy for one of my kind to snap, which I told her as we ambushed her in the dark kitchen. It smelled like heaven then, though I ignored it.

And she didn't scream. It will always sit with me that she looked at me and didn't scream.

Those captivating eyes melted, hardened, and watered for me. I could've done a great many things that night: rightfully returned the debt to her father, assigned her a payment agreement in exchange for my lenience, or forced her into some unsavory aspect of our business. But no, those eyes were all I saw. That soft sigh of relief when she first noticed me in the corner. And so I claimed her for myself.

As my personal chef.

And now I know how blind I've been. I should feel guilty, but I can't. Not when the need of her rages in my blood. My eyes are blurry but they track her specter all the same.

She wears a headscarf, but underneath I can see small, soft-looking, tousled, curls that grow carefree from her crown, perfectly complementing the free-spirited way she cooks and bakes. It's a shame she keeps her hair covered for the most part, but I understand the need to protect it in this harsh environment.

I vaguely recall catching glimpses of her swaying around the fridge, dancing behind the stove, her smile blinding as she worked at the cutting board. I'd like to be the one she dances with like that someday. The image of her in my cell, brushing away damp curls stays with me. As does the look on her face when she watches me. Those slanted thick brows over a gentle oval face. Curved full lips and naturally bright cheeks.

Beautiful eyes, sweeping lashes.

Chef of the best goddamn steak I've ever had in my life. Owner of the juiciest ass I've ever seen. I have never once allowed myself to think of her this way. *Never.* I'd steal my glimpses and subsist on them, denying myself what I realize now was the bond I felt writhing under my skin. It was never this insistent. Never this mind-numbing. But it cannot be undone now, much like whatever has happened to me. That thought is as alarming as the frantic pounding of blood rushing away from where it's needed. This reaction is as inconvenient as it is confusing.

I think of every horrible image I've ever seen, trying to kill the erection that hurts worse than my wounds.

To no avail.

Then I think of the darkening bruise over her throat, and every ounce of lust is replaced by the overwhelming need to break something. How *dare* somebody put their hands on what's mine?

I don't know when I started dreaming of her or how long a guard has been standing in my isolation cell as I visualize Melanie's throat, but then there's a hot prod from a taser, and everything goes dark.

Chapter 6 - Mel

Kalen Crowe is a dead man walking.

He can get in line right behind my father for my revenge because even though he's a goddamn *inmate* with absolutely no rights, the guards listened to him. Leaving me locked in his cell until all the blood beyond the bed was gone.

I could scream, still thinking about the heavy weight of those eyes on me as I worked. Something else inside me demands attention, but I refuse to acknowledge it. I'm so damn mad I would actually rather fight than fuck for once.

Chaz kept asking if I was okay, but what was the point in answering? Not when my arms were so tired I could barely lift them. Sweat made my hands so slick on the brushes I had to eventually strip half of my coveralls.

And when I was finally finished and released from his cell, I couldn't help but palm the pocket with his balled-up note.

I could use the lead even if I ignored the asshole it came from. *If he even had a lead.* By the time the rest of my shift is done, sweat is dripping down my face, and the inside of this uniform is drenched. I smell like damp skin and deodorant that has stretched as far as it'll go. Each time I drag a sleeve over my forehead, the beads of sweat return almost immediately.

Goddamn, what I wouldn't do for a breeze.

And enough medicine to kill this fever. A long shower awaits me when I get home, and just enough sleep to keep me alive before I check in at the restaurant. My best friend, Alice, has been pulling doubles between my restaurant and her day job to cover for me while I'm here. I almost didn't tell her what happened, too ashamed and embarrassed to admit I fell for my father's crap *again*.

But after the restaurant was closed for two days in a row, she didn't give me a chance to hide. Ally showed up at my house with a bottle of my favorite wine and swore I wouldn't get a single sip if I didn't fess up.

I can't even express to her what it means to me. When I try, all I manage is a *thank you* and tears. But what I really mean to say is that I'm so beyond grateful to have someone in my corner. To be able to share my burdens with another person instead of doing it all on my own as I have for years.

Every day that I consider giving up on my dream, I remember her sacrifices, her love for me, and I keep going. It's why I have to finish this task.

The break room is quiet when my coworkers and I return, stripping out of the garish white over-suits and rubber boots. Whoever chose such a color for cleaning the inside of a prison had a terrible sense of humor.

I peel mine off carefully and tuck my prize into my bra before I toss everything into the laundry chute.

Instinctually, my fingers twist around a curl at my temple in an attempt to distract myself from reading the note in front of everyone. My anxiety is running high. What I wouldn't give to just relax at home in my pajamas after a nice, long shower. I need a self-care day or three. With the deepest sigh, I start daydreaming about what I'd do. Probably visit the spa and get a facial like I used to each month. Then, I'd go home and do my nails because I actually find it relaxing and fun. Maybe binge my favorite shows while snacking afterward.

I'm so tired.

My damp curls cling to my forehead and the nape of my neck. At least the orange-scented hair moisturizer overpowers any other scents right now. *Kind of.*

Eventually, I follow behind the others, heading toward the guard station, when a meaty hand wraps around my bicep, jerking me to a stop. As much as it makes me cringe, I can tell who it is based on the hand and grip alone. I groan.

I just want to go home, have a spiked apple cider, eat fresh cookies, and contemplate paying back my father's five hundred-thousand-dollar loan without committing a felony or aiding and abetting a criminal. Oh, and find some time to add in a wash day.

"Dirk," I warn with enough bite that he hesitates to pull me further into his body heat. My first thought is to glance down at the dip in my shirt. Can he see the wad of paper pressed against my flesh?

"Melly, honey, just the girl I was looking for. Got one last job for you tonight."

"It's Melanie, and can't you tell me about the job without touching me?"

"Testy, are we?" He releases me and steps back. "It's alright. Cleaning up after Crowe would put me in a mood, too, Melly. I won't take it personally."

That nickname sizzles as it hits my ears. I *hate* it. He knows I hate it—just like he knows I don't want to be crowded, eye-fucked, or *groped*. He knows because I've made it clear verbally and physically, and yet every other shift, he finds a way to do all three because he knows I won't quit. *Can't* quit. He might not know the details, but he knows enough to push his luck.

The words to put him in his place are on the tip of my tongue when he clarifies, "It's below ground, Melly. Haven't you been wanting more hours? Wanting to work the higher paying cleans? Well, here's your chance. I put a special word just for you. *No, no.* No need to thank me. At least, not before you see the mess you need to clean tonight. Thankfully, you're the best blood cleaner on staff."

I turn to find his trademark greasy smile in place as he ogles. I bite back my frustration and manage to mutter a forced "thanks" through my clenched teeth. "What about Griggs or Shaw? They've been here longer. They've got seniority."

I don't want to add backstabbing my coworkers to my list of things to worry about.

"Griggs is out for medical, and Shaw worked a double last night. I mean, if you don't want it, baby, just say so. You probably won't get another opportunity to prove yourself any time soon." He throws his hands up and turns back the way he came.

"Wait!" My shoulders lock up, my body begging me to leave, even as I nod when he meets my eyes. This is the moment I've been waiting a month for. Too bad it comes with an escort from the guard that can't take a hint. He's too handsy. Too comfortable around me. Too sure I won't knock some sense into him if he tries that shit last week again.

"Let me use the bathroom first." I barely let the words settle before I'm halfway through the bathroom door, fitting myself into a stall. Tugging the paper free, I unfold each edge, careful not to tear it.

My heart soars, then drops. There are only two lines written on the scrap of—what I realize now—is magazine paper.

Lower level truck entrance is unguarded at 3 am.

Who are you? Who sent you?

Hopefully he knows who I am now, and I'm sure he can guess who sent me. Exhaling roughly, I think about the first line. How am I supposed to find the lower level truck entrance? And how the hell am I supposed to get us both there at a specific time?

I ponder the options as I shred the note and flush the pieces.

Dirk is already waiting in front of the service elevator. He quirks a brow upon seeing me exit the break room without an over-suit. It might be strange, but the idea of sweltering inside the material for even one more hour makes my skin crawl. I'd rather ruin these house jeans.

"I can wash my clothes tonight," I say, answering his unasked question.

"Heard Crowe trapped you in his cell," Dirk states as a greeting, bypassing my strange attire. He grabs my supplies to help me carry them. "He couldn't help himself, huh? Man is unhinged."

I don't know what Dirk means until I realize he's looking at my throat and the bruise forming there. I don't bother correcting him. I'm not wasting my breath defending one asshole against another.

Yes, I'm still mad.

"Did you know, after you left, he attacked the guard that released him for mobility? Got himself thrown in isolation for a week."

I swallow roughly. "No, I didn't know that, and it doesn't make any sense. Why attack a guard knowing he would end up in - ?"

Realization slams into me. *Truck loading at 3 am.* He's getting himself put into a lower level. He trusts that I will somehow pull off the impossible. And he trusts that I'll do it *tonight.*

Upon further consideration, Kalen Crowe might actually be an idiot if he thinks I can pull off a great escape this quickly. I don't say any of that to Dirk as he herds me into the small metal carriage and presses the floor number. He doesn't seem to mind that I never reply to his small talk, which is odd, but I'm too busy thinking to care.

The elevator ride down is even hotter than the sticky uniform I'm wearing, and I can't tell if the offensive smell Dirk emits is body odor or something he ate for lunch. Either way it's starting to make my head hurt. He's like a physical repellent. If he would just step back...

A bead of sweat finally breaks free from my hairline, trickling down my temple in a sudden rush that ends beneath my chin.

Thankfully, the doors open a moment later, bringing a slightly mildewy breeze that I welcome.

I almost stumble over myself when I spot what appears to be a loading zone down the hallway. My heart races as I store the information away for later.

Dirk is already three doors down, and I jog to catch up. At the fifth door, he stops to swipe his pass over it. For the first time, I realize that isolation cells look exactly how they sound. There are at least a dozen doors lining each side of the hall, but all around them are solid concrete. As the door to room number five slides open, I am met with an overwhelming darkness.

A void that seems to stretch on forever stares back at me. My body tenses, and the hairs on my neck stand up as a feeling of unease creeps over me. It's as if I'm being watched by someone or something lurking beyond that impenetrable veil of blackness.

"Here," Dirk hands me my supplies and a flat case that looks like it opens. "You'll need this to see."

"What the hell do you mean '*I'll need this to see*?!'" I snap. "If you think I'm going into that dark ass cell with no idea what's even in there, you've lost your mind."

"Why do you think these cleaners get paid so much more, Melly?" He deadpans, staring at me like I'm an idiot. Okay, he does have a point, but still. I must look stupid if he thinks I'd take a job like that. No thanks.

"Look, the prisoner is restrained. *This* will help you see. Just open it and point it at the ceiling. When you're finished, press the buzzer near the door, and I'll let you out."

He says it like that's not the wildest set of instructions I've ever heard. Like I wouldn't be inside a cell with whatever restrained prisoner they paired me with. Absolutely no way in hell—

"*Let me out*?" I snap, my heart rate climbing with my volume. "If it's so safe, then why can't you leave the damn door open? Fuck no."

I've almost stepped out of his reach when Dirk roughly grabs me by the back of my neck and shoves me beyond the doorway. The hiss that escapes is involuntary. One part shock at the audacity, and one part pain. Each of his fingers pressed the tender skin over my bruise.

My supplies clatter to the floor, along with whatever he gave me to see. They disappear into the darkness. This is a horror I've never imagined. Raw terror climbs up my throat at the savage growl ripping through the dark. There's some kind of animal in here.

"I don't have time for this shit, Melanie, ring the buzzer when you're done." He snaps as I land on my knees. "And don't growl at me, *fucker*," he shouts into the darkroom, just beyond me, "or I won't be gentle next time."

And before I can scramble toward the door, it's already sliding closed. The sound of the lock engaging fills my body with ice, pulling some pathetic sound out of me.

But the voice, the one that swallows the darkness between us, fills my body with heat, and the tension strangling my heart eases just a fraction.

"Melanie," Kalen Crowe says like he might rule the very darkness we're suspended in. "Don't be afraid. I won't hurt you."

Chapter 7 - Kalen

*F*uck.

It's my first coherent thought, and it has nothing to do with the pounding behind my eyes. Or the chafing on my wrists that says I've been hanging by these chains for a while. It has everything to do with the throbbing between my legs. As if my awareness only makes my cock worse, it kicks forward, leaking across my stomach and the tops of my thighs.

For a moment, I think I must've been stripped while I was out. It's not the first time they've tried to hose me down when I bled too much. But as my awareness slowly trickles into the rest of my narrow world, I realize the jumpsuit I tied around my waist has loosened, slipping slightly down on my hips.

I blink. Black. Everywhere.

Then, something scuttles across the floor. There are no rats in my normal cell. I've barely registered that I'm in isolation when my second coherent thought settles.

It smells like Melanie.

And nearby, something sounds like her, too.

Carefully, I turn toward the open door that barely illuminates anything beyond the two figures—one, a petite woman whose curls are saturated in her delicious scent. The mildew-coated breeze is overrun with her scent - oranges, red currant, and cream. The chains groan. I hadn't even realized I was reaching for her until the metal hisses against the concrete. The one who stands with her is a guard I've always hated. He's slimy and underhanded, the worst kind of man because he cannot be trusted.

Not to mention, he wielded the whip that shredded my back only hours ago. The thought of those hands near Melanie nearly pulls a feral growl from my chest.

And then he *shoves her* into the cell, whatever items in her hands clattering to the ground around her. That rips the sounds free. If I hadn't already decided on his demise, that action would have sealed it. My wrists chafe against the cuffs. She needs me. If any part of her is hurt...

"I don't have time for this shit, Melanie, ring the buzzer when you're done." He snaps from beyond the cell, a dead man talking. "And don't growl at me, *fucker*, or I won't be gentle next time."

He has no idea how *not gentle* his death will be. There's a toxin that Ankylos can flood into our claws—one that paralyzes. Personally, I've never had the ability, or rather, I just never knew how, no matter how much I tried. Knox used to laugh and lord it over me that he, as my younger brother, could do it with ease.

"Maybe the ability skips a sibling," he'd tease when we were pre-teens, experiencing Ankylos puberty and the unique traits it came with.

"Maybe intelligence skips a sibling," I'd bite back. And we'd playfight, half-serious.

But, since being in this prison and subject to all sorts of stress and pain, I'm beginning to think this experience has changed me not only mentally but physically.

If the pulsing within my hands is to be believed, combined with the new length of my claws themselves, I suspect I have the power to fill them with toxins as well.

The guard had better pray that I don't have that kind of time when I find him alone. Thoughts of his impending doom freeze in their tracks as the door slides closed, locking us in the horrible dark. I hear her whimper.

"Melanie." I attempt to whisper, but it comes out with far more base, as I barely keep a leash on my temper. "Don't be afraid. I won't hurt you." *Could never hurt her.*

She says nothing at first. The only sound is her panicked breaths.

"It's just me. I swear it."

Then I hear something slide along the floor. Maybe her foot? A wafting breeze of hers fills my lungs, and I groan. There's no suppressing it, whether it's appropriate or not. I can't help the building ache.

"Kalen?" She whispers, panic coating her words. "Is it really you? Are you alright?"

I'm not prepared for what hearing my name from her lips does to me. She's always remained professional, referring to me as my family name. With just my murmured name, I'm making a mess all over my jumpsuit, my skin, and the bed. Fresh wetness glides down one of my thighs, my cock kicking all over the place. It's like going through maturity all over again. Only I'm not alone where I can easily hide my raging hormones.

I blow out the tensest breath known to man and think of horrors, festering wounds, misery, and my greatest failures—*anything* to quell the fire in my veins. I quietly thank the heavens for the dark.

"It's me," I assure her, clearing the hoarse want out of my throat. "Can you follow my voice?"

I don't want her terrified in the dark, wondering if something awful is about to attack her. And if the guard comes back, I want her near me. The tight cuffs on my wrists beg the question of how I plan to protect her. But I'll figure it out, whatever the cost.

Things skitter across the floor as she finds her way through the dark. She's listening to me, crawling to me, entrusting me with her safety...

There's no hope of wrangling my cock under control now. It's too monumental a task when every ounce of my brain is occupied with the woman scooting across the filthy floor.

"Good girl, Melly, keep going. Follow the sound of my voice. You're almost here."

"I - I," she starts, sounding caught off guard by my praise. She clears her throat and begins again, her tone much more confident and stern. "*I hate that nickname.*"

My vision in the dark is only slightly better than a human's, but not by much. Still, I can hear her closeness. I can smell the increase of her scent in the air. And I grin at her hard-ass response. So resilient. "Noted Melanie," I tell her, my voice a silkier purr than I would like.

No part of me considers that I'm half naked. Nor do I think of the erection that would be obvious if she accidentally touched me—the lubricant coating most of my lower half. And worst of all, I don't consider how bloody I am until she curses just beyond the bed.

"It smells like blood in here," she hisses. "What am I supposed to clean?"

My back, I think uselessly. That can't happen. Coughing around the thought of her hands on my skin, I manage to whisper, "Not sure, but it's not important now. If the smell is unpleasant, cover your nose. I can't be sure you're safe until you're beside me. Come closer."

"It's ... it's not unpleasant," she says quietly. "Under the copper, there's something earthy. Refreshing. Almost comforting. Does that make sense?" It sounds like she shakes her head. "Never mind, I've probably been doing this job for too long already if blood is any kind of comfort. I'm really just concerned. I was worried you were hurt."

"Not hurt ... badly," I lie, words failing me after her admission. Does it make sense that her *mate's* blood soothes her? *Yes.* If she only knew how her natural instincts were driving her toward solidifying the bond. I didn't know humans were susceptible to the pull, but I'm thrilled to know we both feel it.

My body begs me to show her exactly how comforting I can be, utterly under her spell. I'm so lost in my own craving that I don't notice she's made it up to the bed until a tentative touch slides across my stomach.

"What does 'not hurt *badly*' mean, Crowe?" The firm tone is almost enough to distract me from her hand on my skin.

I flinch and shudder. "Don't —" I barely get the word out before she's gasping.

"You are hurt!" She exclaims, both hands now exploring the damp abdominal muscles that lead to where I'm throbbing for her. Searching. Searing. Teasing. Whatever the heavens are made of — her smile, those curls, her doe eyes — this is hell. Having her so close and being unable to touch her in return.

"Not ... blood ..." I grit, trembling under the warm softness of her fingers. I tug at the bonds above, straining. She doesn't understand what she's doing, but the chains groan with me. They understand how I'm being bent out of shape around her.

Heavens above, she has to stop.

"Not blood?" Melanie scoffs. "You think I don't know what warm blood feels like? My hands are sliding all over you. You're covered, Kalen."

"*Don't* talk about your hands sliding over me," I warn.

I can't bring myself to tell her to stop touching me, even if I'm about a minute away from embarrassing myself worse than I already am. I can feel my balls drawing tight, tensing. She must hear something in my voice because her attention shifts.

Her touch slows, slipping through the proof of what she does to me. Just her scent. Her voice. The thought of her in my mind. What it might be like to touch her. It undoes me little by precious little. She moves slightly lower, testing me, carefully working out the words I know are on her tongue.

"You're not bleeding?" She asks, her voice lower and rougher than it was. Each time I think I cannot be more attracted to her, I am immediately proven wrong.

"Not there." I swallow as she lifts one hand. In the dark, my heightened hearing catches the rub of her fingers, testing the fluid. I almost combust.

"Then what — "

"*Melanie*," I plead for some kind of mercy as I hear her raise that hand toward her face, scenting me. The earthy comfort, as she called it. The scent of her mate.

Of my arousal.

More leaks free. I'm done for. Everything I've achieved in my life, and I'm going to die right here before I've ever laid a hand on my mate.

"It's you," she says, inhaling again. "It's been you this whole time."

I don't know what she means to say; I hardly hear her at all over the sound of my pounding heart. But it's lost somewhere in translation as her free hand rejoins the other. Lower still on my stomach. Then, they both freeze.

"Sorry, I don't ... I shouldn't touch you without permission," she says, sounding as embarrassed about her instinctive actions as I am about coating us both in my rampant desire.

"At this point, if you stop touching me, I don't think I'll survive." It's horribly needy of me, but I cannot lie. Not right now. Not to her. I'm fumbling through this as I did through my maturing amongst humans and my creation of The Divide. I've butchered many moments with my nature. This is no different. It's indelicate and primal, nothing like what I've heard it's supposed to be. There should be courting and sweet declarations. Some physical proof of a male's ability to protect.

Not *this* mindless, desperate craving. Embarrassing myself with the eagerness to cum. Mating instincts have never been a factor for me. My Ankylos schoolmates used to say I was a late bloomer, or that I wouldn't bloom at all because I seemed to lack pheromones or pleasure spikes like them. I've never had so much lubricant for a joining. I've never considered what it would be like to do this the right way.

I hardly scented her at all. I overlooked the details that would have confirmed what she was to me months ago.

Maybe my manhood has changed like the rest of me. *Stop thinking about it, dammit.*

It happens again, a small release that I can't control. It's close enough to her hand that it must have touched her. Melanie shivers. Honestly, shivers like my arousal is hers, like it's reaching under her skin, too.

It's all new to me, a reminder of how I've been altered, changed due to the warden and his cronies' actions. Although, in this brief, tiny moment, I don't hate the changes.

My scales, though few, now emit a heavy pheromone, the earthy scent of vetiver mixed with bergamot that she loves. Doubling. Drowning her in it. She has me by the tip of my cock, covered with enough fluid to make fitting easier. Something feral comes from my chest at the thought of fitting inside her. *Pressing, forcing, thrusting.*

The sound doesn't startle her, but Melanie's nails dig into my flesh. She has me by the throat. By the balls. By every rational thought in my head. I might cum before she touches the throbbing parts of me.

She hums. *Hums.*

Something low and husky. Full of want. As if what's happening makes any sense. As if she knows exactly what she's touching now. The brittle hope that she might want to —

When her tentative fingers find their way under my open jumpsuit, my back arches violently. A groan escapes my lips as I turn away from her, trying to contain the intense pleasure that radiates through my body. I focus on taking steady breaths, so I don't subconsciously hold it in.

It's embarrassing, and I know it's a far cry from who I've been the entire time she's known me. Ruthless. Calculated. Brisk.

I know full well how I now appear. I'm panting, sharp fangs pressing into my tongue too hard. I might even be trembling. I know it, and yet I can't stop because when Melanie presses her palm around the base of my cock, my whole body lifts off the bed. Her touch is a brand.

"Can I ... ?" She trails off, her voice low, her breathing labored. She's fumbling blindly, unable to see, and somehow, it's even more erotic than if she had grabbed me outright.

Melanie wants to explore. To play and pleasure and tease. *Me.*

She's asking if she can touch *me. My* cock, that hasn't stopped weeping for her all day.

"*Please.* Y-yes."

I'm not above begging when the pressure, the desire, is too intense to resist. I tell her as much as she finds the head. Every thought is wiped from my mind. There's no shyness on her end, and for me, there are only embarrassing moans I'm not too proud to emit.

She rolls her hand around, gripping, testing, exploring.

A long swipe of the slick head with her thumb elicits a bowed back. A short stroke over a particularly sensitive ridge has me hissing and clenching my fists hard enough to force the claws in my nail beds to lengthen. Does she feel the parts of my anatomy that are framed around her pleasure? Ridges and roping veins that throb. The knot that aches. The parts that want to slide home and ...

She grips me roughly, just the way I like to be held. My head is swimming, and without sight, every other sense is going haywire. She starts pressing the raised points on the shaft more firmly, tugging at the skin with each pass. I'm nearly blind. Dizzy. Suddenly, she's fisting the entire base, grasping my knot, and my balls draw tighter, too full and hypersensitive. Overwhelmed by the intense sensation. One hand trails over a soaked thigh, then back up the tightly woven muscles just above where she strokes.

I don't even think she realizes what she's doing. It seems like she's lost in her instincts, not even realizing how deeply she's leaning into them. Our scents mix together, along with the sensation of our skin pressed against each other. This bond between us grows stronger with each passing moment, as if it's part of some natural order. We're becoming one even as I feel like falling apart.

"Mel – Melanie, I'm," the words I try to say are drowned by the roar of release that shoots down my spine. Literally and figuratively. It comes out of nowhere and everywhere. Then it's on her, marking her soft skin, and the thought takes the last of my senses.

I give everything over to pleasure. Shuddering as the scales across my skin harden, and morph, each producing a single spike in an attempt to protect my body because this euphoria makes me vulnerable. I cannot properly defend myself when I'm lost in the feeling of her, when I don't know which way is up or down.

When I can't figure out how to *stop* cumming.

My cock kicks again and again, the throbbing ecstasy moving throughout my body like a single pulse. And then I hear it. *Silence.* Not a single sound. She's even holding her breath.

"M-Melanie," I manage, shuddering. *Get a goddamn grip.*

"Hmm?" She sounds off. As my awareness slowly returns, I realize her hands are no longer on me. She's still holding her breath. I finally gather the last of my senses when I hear her scooting away.

Once. *Twice.*

"What's wrong?" Instantly, I'm on alert, trying to figure out if anything in my cum is toxic to humans. Obviously, we're a compatible species if my parents were hybrid humans themselves. But this place has changed me. The warden's sadistic experiments have forcibly awoken more of my sleeping Drakon genetics. If I've hurt her...

"*Melanie*, what's wrong?"

"Noth—*ughh*," she moans, and it sounds like she falls backward.

What the fuck was that? A husky chuckle slips out of me before I can stop it. Is she blissed out? Giving in to her mating instincts? She's not hurt, that's for sure.

"It's not... *oh god*... funny, Kalen," she hisses.

The laugh slips free again. "Poor little mate," I tease, now that she's eased the distracting pressure from my body, and I know she isn't in pain. I'm still hard and desperate to touch her, but I no longer feel out of my mind.

She growls at me and chokes on the sound. It's adorable and arousing at the same time.

"Are you feeling needy, Melanie?"

"Try having someone cum all over you and see how you feel afterward," she snaps, frustrated with her own body, I assume. Her words paint a delicious picture, though.

"Sounds perfect. Bring that ass back over here."

There was silence before she spoke, low-voiced, "I'm sure you'd like that."

"I would," I confirm.

I hear her scoff, but there's no malice in it. I imagine her playfully rolling her eyes.

Experimentally, I shift my shoulders and discover my back is completely fine. Thanks to my alien ancestry, the wounds have closed, and the skin will heal without a mark. To my satisfaction, the metal cuffs begin to bend as I tug. Mating just might get us out of here faster.

We're leaving tonight, I decided. I can't allow my mate to remain in a place like this any longer. None of the hybrids down here with me can stay here anymore either. We're all going home.

"And you poked me with one of those damn *spikes*," she hisses. If she grits her teeth any harder, they'll crack. I'm about to tell her as much when what she says starts unraveling in my head. *Spikes?*

"Did it break your skin, Melanie?" The laugh is barely contained as I imagine her writhing on the floor, her body pulsing with need. For me. Because if there's one thing I know for certain, it's that during mating, those spikes are full of a potent pleasure hormone. If they're strong to my kind, there's no telling how drugged her human body would be. She might cum right there on the floor at just the suggestion of me filling her up.

I'm so close to saying it—

"Ye–*ugh, oh my god*," she tries and fails to communicate.

"My poor, horny little human," I tease her, my voice dropping into a dangerously low register. Lust consumes me, every second filled with thoughts of her desires and the wetness I know is waiting for me. Whatever was started has begun to build again. She's aching. I can smell her natural scent deepening in the air. *Drenched*.

"Do you want me to make you feel better, Melanie?"

Chapter 8 – Mel

"**Y**-you can call me M-Mel. if you want."

As the words slip free, I realize they're not what I meant to say at all. I don't care what he calls me. Not when there's fire flowing through every vein in my body. It radiates from the puncture near my palm.

Fuck.

I've been so distracted by the sounds he emits that I hadn't noticed his thrashing until it was too late - until something needle-sharp stabbed my palm. Quickly, I drew back my hand, but it was already too late.

"Mel," he tests, still out of breath and his voice thick with pleasure. "I said, get your ass back over here. I can help make it better."

"After what just happened, it's only right to use my nickname," I laugh bitterly, ignoring him. I *can't* go back over there. I'm not even sure I can stand. "I mean, I hardly know you at all. Unless you count knowing how your dick feels."

He lets out a slow grunt in acknowledgment of my words, and the sound is an aphrodisiac. Or maybe it's his cum still covering my hands. It's so *warm*. And I have the strangest urge to rub it over myself. My thin t-shirt is damp with sweat once more, and there are beads of it over every inch of me. I think his cum is making the heat worse.

I think it's making me crazy. I feel so close to an orgasm it hurts.

My mind keeps replaying the moan of pleasure that broke free when he tumbled over the edge. The one that sounded an awful lot like my name. Like a plea. It might have been the most erotic thing I've ever heard. His voice was hoarse and raw, vulnerable and so blissed out that I was actually jealous.

I'm *not* anymore.

My body is a live wire. I don't know if it's the dark that gave me the freedom to explore him like I've longed to or the warm, refreshing scent of Kalen that fills my lungs. It's unlike anything I've ever experienced. Unlike perfume in how far into my body the intoxicating scent seems to reach, twisting my stomach, clenching my core.

I wish I could've seen his face, or the color that his flushed dick turned when my hands brought him over the edge. What had just occurred between my boss and I was unlike any sensation I'd felt before, and too much of my mind was trying to form a mental image.

And now the incessant throbbing in my palm slowly begins to radiate all over my body, sensitizing my skin. My breath stutters as I realize it was *him*.

This whole time, it was the smell of his skin, of the warm liquid drying over my skin. In his cell, haunting me at home after my shifts...

It takes a monumental effort not to lift my damp fingers to my lips, even in the dark that feels like too far. Like I've lost myself somewhere between fear and lust. I'm directionless. Confused.

I want more.

"*Mel*," he growls, pulling a wanton moan from me from somewhere deep. Somewhere that hasn't been touched in a very, very long time. "Yes, mate, there you are. Come *here*."

Mate. Why does he call me that? I hated my father for the possibility that he sold me into a mating. And yet my body moves of its own free will. I don't feel the ground I crawl over, just the rough brush of my jeans in the few moments it takes me to get back to the bed.

There's still a hint of blood in the air, but it's lessened immensely.

As I pull myself up to the bed, my body shuts down. The moan that pulls free is devastating and humiliating. There's a metallic whine and thud before strong arms are lifting me.

It hurts. God, I'm dying of so much incomplete pleasure it *hurts*. I thrash against the arms, my skin so sensitive I want to scream.

I don't even consider how he got out of his bindings.

"Shh," Kalen soothes. He smells warm and fragrant. His scent gets richer the closer I am. It makes my nipples throb. I'm leaking between the layers of fabric, *drenched*. "I'll help you."

"What's wrong with me?" I whine, so uncomfortable my body starts to twist out of his hold. He clamps me down against his warmth, his damp skin. If he's heaven, the slick glide against his bare skin is hell. I *want* it. Over me. Inside me. Underneath me. Everywhere.

There's a ridge of what must be a jumpsuit where his hips meet mine. Thinking of how I just slipped my hand beneath to stroke the still-hard length makes me want to come apart, slip out of my skin, and into his.

It's bizarre and overwhelming, and I *need* more.

"It's the bond," he says. His voice is calm, though, for me, the undercurrent of lust is ratcheting into oblivion now that our damp bodies are touching.

"Bond? What does that mean? And why - why do you keep calling me mate? We didn't enter a contract." I'm hazy, my mind focused on the shirt that is rubbing against my nipples, and my swollen clit that throbs, reminding me of its existence. "Don't most alien hybrids *usually* choose to mate amongst each other?"

He sighs, and I feel his breath against my damp shirt. He must know the effect it's going to have because his fingers are already soothing my nipples, rubbing in slow circles until the buds are warm and tight, aching for a mouth or the wet tip of his dick to drag along it. My clit throbs harder, and I pant. "This will help," he says softly. "Let me help."

Yes, help me.

I get the sense that helping me cum is as much a need for him as a relief for me, so I gamble a little. "Answer my questions, or I'll stop letting you touch me."

His growl is small and nonthreatening, and so is my threat.

"The warden has been experimenting with hybrids under his care. He's subjected me to constant stress and deadly experiments. I've had to literally fight for my life being here."

"Oh my God!" I whisper, horrified and stunned. "Wait, the warden did this to you? Warden Gunther?"

"*Gunther!*" Kalen exclaims as if he hadn't remembered the man's name. After a moment, he seems to remember his point. "I don't know his aim exactly. But the constant threat of pain and death has triggered the awakening of at least *some* of my dormant

Drakon DNA. I've been more feral, more primal, more instinctual. And your scent has been far more potent than normal."

"And now you're fully mated to a human? To *me*?" He presses my tight nipples harder, rough like the thought excited him as much as it excited me.

"Not fully." The *not yet* is hardly subtle, and neither is the way my body slicks, preparing for the rest. The thought makes my head spin. He hasn't even asked if being mated to him is what I want. The small, wounded part of me whispers that I've always wanted this. That it would be wonderful to have a man in my life who wouldn't betray me or carelessly disappoint me.

Or intentionally hurt me for no good reason at all.

"We can discuss this later once we're back at my home. For now, if we're making our escape tonight, we'll need you fully functional. Can I ... er ... do I have your permission to please you?"

The nod is so jerky and quick I'm surprised he sees it, let alone understands it before his hand dives, *dives* between my worn jeans and skin. His fingers glide over the slickness, and his groan is obscene, laced with the things he'd like to do.

"I will not fuck my mate in a prison cell. I *will not fuck my mate in a prison cell,*" he repeats, convincing himself not to do exactly what I want.

His thumb trails a circle over my clit, and my body jolts. His face is buried in my neck, breathing me in. I haven't had a chance to go home and shower today yet. And being someone who's pretty big on hygiene, this upsets me. Inwardly, I'm kicking myself, suddenly feeling insecure and embarrassed. I freeze under his touch.

"D-don't, I —" I started, trying to pull away. His fingers play with my opening as his thumb picks up the pace. "I've been working all day."

He exhales over my throat, jerking me closer. "You smell *divine*," he whispers—something hot and wet, *and entirely too long*, drags over my neck from collarbone to ear tip. The tip of his thumb increases its pressure, and I feel the smallest prick of sharpness. A claw? Before I can understand, two fingers thrust inside me. They curve toward his thumb, pressing along my inner wall with the same prick of sharpness — pleasure on the razor edge of pain.

I let out a strangled moan, surprising even myself.

"*Fuck*, you like the claws, don't you?" His voice is hot liquid rushing over my body "I love that you trust me with them against your most vulnerable parts."

I moan at the mix of soft pads and sharp nails. They're driving me higher. So high I almost don't realize he's kissing my neck, my jaw, my cheeks. I turn my head, and then he's dipping into my mouth, tasting like heat.

"You need more," he says between presses. "I'll give you what you need."

His tongue forces mine to move, guiding us into a sloppy, wet glide that matches what he's doing below. I can sense there's more of his tongue that he's keeping to himself. The wet drag against my throat is far longer than what's in my mouth.

I want the rest. I want to choke and scream and claw and maybe even *die* a little with the orgasm threatening to bowl me over. Where are these thoughts coming from?

Mate. He growls and clutches me tighter as if he can hear the word echoing inside my brain.

My body moves on its own, matching the pace of his fingers with thrusts and grinds that mimic what I'd do to the length trapped between us. I'm close to begging for it, needing to work around something that stretches me wide.

But he thrusts another finger, three now working me over, my jeans suddenly wide open and pulled down to my thighs. The sounds his fingers make on my skin. The sounds he's pressing into my mouth. The hand he locks around my head so I can't pull away.

I'm—I'm—

He thrusts the full length of his tongue into my throat until I choke. My whole body clenches. He pulls back with a hoarse groan, but I'm scrambling for more. I reach for his shoulders, begging, and his tongue is down my throat again.

There are too many sensations. The prick from his spike in my palm is now giving way to the most overwhelming, tingling heat I've ever felt. It's in my muscles and veins, my blood. It's everywhere. And as I gag around his tongue, I feel myself tip over the edge.

Bliss rockets out of me. And as I scream into his chest, I lose all sense of reason. My body tenses to the point of pain, riding out every single molecule that's exploding inside my body. The sounds. Maybe I lose my hearing for a moment because I can't hear my own moans of pleasure until he roars into my neck, curling protectively around me. Then the sound comes back all at once, drowning me in the masculine moans he's kissing into my skin.

If his first orgasm was anything like mine, I don't know how he can manage to cum again, but he does. I feel the press of wet heat from below as my body continues to spiral into another peak.

It's unending, overwhelming, *perfect*. The orgasm to end all others. It feels like warming under the sun, the slide of cool water over a parched throat, a taut muscle being stretched *just right*.

I can't speak or move anymore, just a boneless body being held up by my alien mate. And he's panting, shaking like he can't bear any more pleasure either.

"I can't wait to get you home," he mumbles, pressing a damp kiss to my forehead. I can't properly care for you here, but soon. *Soon*."

Chapter 9 – Mel

There's something particularly insane about a guy tearing down an isolation door — one that has been welded and bolted into place. One that easily weighs more than me.

And when I say *tear*, I mean it. His fist goes through the metal with a crunch that makes my stomach sink. I've hardly wrapped my mind around the broken chain cuffs dangling from each wrist when the glint of a hallway light first breaches the room. The sound of tearing metal grates in the back of my mind, and again, I'm reminded that I don't really know how safe I am with Crowe. I *feel* safe, but that doesn't mean much. I have a terrible sense of self-preservation. Case in point.

Another punch through the metal makes a horrible crunch that startles me. I think it's the bones in his wrist or forearm until he shrugs his arm free without a wince and grabs the free edge. The metal is warped, and he somehow rips an entire seam from the hole to the corner. Then he repeats the motion three more times until it's been peeled apart crudely like a can.

I can't wrap my mind around it.

When he reaches his hand back to ensure I'm following, the light catches. The hand is covered in scrapes and metal shavings, but none of the small wounds are bleeding too badly. I notice spikes protruding from his knuckles and make a mental note to avoid them. I have no idea how they work, but I don't want to take any chances and accidentally inject myself with his potent hormones again.

We don't have that kind of time, though my body pulses with reminders of what just occurred. Actually, it's a miracle that I'm upright at all — that I'm in this situation. That I have a *mate*... My thoughts start to spiral. With my luck, this is yet another mistake. Yet I can't help how my body gravitates to him. How I feel safest when he's near. How, even in this awful situation, one he unknowingly put me in, I don't hate him for it. Maybe I never truly did.

"Mel, let's go," he speaks firmly, but there is no trace of anger in his voice. It's almost as if he understands that I need time to gather my thoughts. Truth is, I haven't exactly processed every-thing yet. "Mel, we need to leave now!" he says again, urging me to snap out of it. My attention shifts to him, and he grabs my wrist, tugging me into the dull hallway light. I freeze. I don't even think I can breathe until a ragged gasp tears from my throat.

His back.

Kalen throws a look over his shoulder, his brow raised. But I can't focus on his handsome face. Nor can I think about how long this hallway will remain empty so we can safely traverse it. All I see is how Kalen's ruined jumpsuit, loosely tied around his waist, exposes his back covered in huge angry red marks crusted with blood - wounds that were once opened - now almost healed.

"*What* happened?" I ask, feeling a lump in my throat. I struggle to wrap my head around it. *How ...? Why...?*

If the fresh-looking blood on the back of his jumpsuit was anything to go by, Kalen's injuries hadn't happened too long ago. Meaning that when I came across him tonight, he had been hurt badly, far worse than he let on. The intimate moment we had shared together flashes in my mind, and I marvel over how Kalen managed to find any relief, any pleasure at all, in his painful condition.

What was the reason for injuries like this? Why did ProMaxim staff normalize inmate injuries and death so much? Was the extra torture and pain necessary for those already incarcerated and condemned to this place?

The anger that floods my body is overwhelming, but still, I wait for his answer as to what the hell happened to him.

"There are real monsters out there, Mel," Kalen says, snarling, his long fangs fully on display for the first time in my presence.

"And some of the prison staff are among them, that's what. That's why we have to hurry. I need to get the others out of here."

I shiver both because of his words and his expression. He's pissed. Understandably so.

"The others...," my voice trails. "Of course. B-but how - why would you let me do *any* of that if you were in this much pain?" That nasty guilt is building. How could I be so self-centered? Why did I ignore the smell of blood or what I was sent into his cell for?

Oh my God. I took advantage of him. Sure he was my boss on the outside. But in here ... he was just another prisoner.

I feel sick.

I'm no better than ...

"Mel," he says carefully, bumping me out of my spiraling thoughts, as if he somehow knew I was moments away from losing my mind. "Take a breath. There was no pain, I promise you. And being with you, my mate, sped up the healing. My wounds will heal entirely soon. So don't worry. We didn't do anything *I* didn't want." He suddenly looks concerned, checking me over as if looking for something. "How 'bout you? Are you alright?"

His hand, the same one that could tear steel off a frame, is gentle as he caresses my cheek, surprising me with its tenderness. I bask in his touch.

"I'm okay, given the circumstances," I tell him reassuringly, and I lift my hand to cover his. In the darkness of that room back there, Kalen hadn't done anything I'd protest to either. He did nothing I wouldn't do again under better circumstances.

"Good."

"But, I could use a long shower ... and maybe a strong drink," I add, partially because it's true and partially to humor him.

He manages a small smile. "Right then. Let's go. You can wash up, and we'll talk over drinks later, I promise."

His tone, though firm, is kind. My heart skips a beat. I swallow thickly and nod.

Then we're moving, and I'm briefly distracted by his horns. Were they always this big? They're impressive—curved and add nearly a foot to his height. Despite being confined to this prison for the past few months, Kalen's in better shape than I imagined. He's hardly broken a sweat. I'm barely able to keep up. I can't help but wonder again what Kalen looks like beneath his jumpsuit.

"Wait here," he commands quickly, looking down both paths of the hallway before disappearing inside a room. It dawns on me that I have no idea where he's taken me. I'd never been in this area of the prison before, and admittedly, he distracted me on the way here. Kalen's always been magnetic, with a gift for easily drawing people in. It's probably one of the skills that helped him recruit his current workforce. His loyal foot soldiers who helped him take over the city's underground crime syndicates, dismantling them and creating The Divide in their wake. Still, he kept most people at arm's length.

Although he knew how to command a room, and charm a crowd, Kalen came off to me as a guarded individual, who could project an air of unapproachability with ease. While I had cooked for him and his entourage in the past, I couldn't help but notice there seemed to be just a select few friends and associates whom he trusted, whom he'd genuinely open up to.

I want to know him. The thought enters my mind before I can stop it. I want him to know *me*.

I feel exhilarated by it and slightly scared all the same.

A muffled shout echoes from the room where Kalen disappeared, followed by a series of thumps. The sound is loud enough to reach me through the reinforced metal doors, forcing me to assume that bodies were slamming into the walls. Each passing second adds to the growing worry in my chest as I wait for Kalen to reemerge. When he finally does, I am taken aback by the amount of fresh blood splattered across his torso and covering his claws.

He says nothing before crossing the hall and heading for the nearest door. With a quick tug, it slides open revealing a dimly lit cell. Hesitantly, a male hybrid steps into the hallway light. He has thick ridges extending over his bald head. They travel down his neck, ending in something clipped over the back of both shoulder blades. Instantly I remember the thin wings on the back of that other male hybrid, and wondered if they were the same alien hybrid species.

"You're free," Kalen grunts, taking the male's focus from me and the hall. "Can you scent mark?"

The male before Kalen growls dangerously, revealing upper and lower canines as his mouth drips with saliva.

"Veloc, can you fucking *scent* mark?" Kalen says louder, taking another step into the male's space. I don't think Kalen is familiar with every hybrid within this prison, so I assume Veloc is a hybrid species like Ankylos. It's one I don't recognize.

The angry prisoner nods, then locks eyes with me. "Her. I can scent mark her." His voice is sandpaper-dry and sharp. Kalen's answering growl is just as difficult on my ears. I barely suppress and flinch.

"I don't scent fucking males," the Veloc insists. "And I would never debase myself by scenting an Ankylos prick. Not after I heard one in this very prison killed one of my kind yesterday. ... You wouldn't know who that was, would you?"

"I didn't *want* to. It wasn't by choice."

"The *hell* it wasn't." The other man spat.

The two exchange a heated look, silently daring each other to start a physical confrontation.

"The female, or nothing at all. And don't worry, I don't want your fucking mate."

He can tell?

"Fine. I'm sure I don't have to explain why we all need to get out of here." Kalen says, at last, his face one atom removed from ice. In a quick movement, he snatches my shirt up and tears the lower half clean off, leaving me in a torn midriff. A flash of tense remorse passes over his face before he turns to the male once more. "The cells are unlocked. Take this, and help release the others. Scent mark it back to the headquarters of The Divide."

The Veloc lifts the scrap of cotton to his nose and inhales. "We'll be given sanctuary even if we refuse to join?"

Kalen nods. "Under my orders. I have a lieutenant who is anticipating you all. You'll be safe, and you can leave anytime. "

The male seems to reassess Kalen, taking him in as if deciding whether he can trust him.

Just then, a siren begins to wail, and all the lights change to a harsh, flashing red.

"Shit. Now Veloc," Kalen snarls. "We'll release this way. You go that way. Head toward loading when you've released everyone you can. The prisoner hardly nods before he runs down the opposite hall.

"Come on, let's hope Knox took care of his end," says Kalen as he leads me through the halls. Each door we pass is tugged open by one of us, and hybrids of every kind are slowly emerging from their rooms. Surprisingly, they follow us, warily forming a small crowd. That's why it takes a minute for Kalen's words to penetrate.

"Wait, Knox? He's expecting you? How can he be expecting you to break out when *I* didn't even know I was going to help you break out until that note?"

"This was always the plan, Mel," he says, like it makes perfect sense. "I came here to break these hybrids out under the suspicion that the prison was housing a secret. Knox's part of the plan is to wait nearby until the sirens go off. He'll be expected to provide a distraction while we all escape. I've got a guy who owns a truck. He'll pick up the prisoners and take them to safety."

He looks back at me when I start to stumble.

"So why the hell am I here, Crowe?" I yell. Anger surges through me. If they had planned this all along, then I never needed to be here in the first place! The sirens blare louder, and I see hybrids scurrying around us, rushing towards what I assume is the dock. From my position, I can just make out the opening where they are headed. "Why would Knox force me to take this job? Why would he give me an ultimatum that I had to come help you break out of prison, or I'd lose everything?"

Shaken up and distressed, I stop in my tracks. I'm reconsidering everything now. Kalen's eyes widen with a mix of confusion and disbelief. I can't tell what it's supposed to mean. Can he not handle a woman standing up for herself? Or is he just shocked that I have some backbone against their deceit? I mean, he and his brother endangered my life for a whole damn month, and for what? To break out Kalen and the others, which they already had a solid plan for that never required my presence?

Why drag me into this? Why allow me to go through all this shit? After everything I've already been through in my life. God. I just want peace.

My eyes well up with unshed tears.

Kalen leans down to meet my height. "Say that again," he whispers almost threateningly, audible despite the loud sirens and the disgruntled hybrid fleeing. "'Knox made you do *what*?"

Instead of repeating myself, I continue my point. "How do you think I ended up here, Kalen? Why would a chef come to work *here* of all places ... and as a *cleaner*?! You knew, you damn bastard! The second you saw me, you had to know that Knox sent me. Why!" I yell and pound my fists against the muscular wall of his chest, attempting to push him away from me to stop him from crowding me. I just want to find my car and go the fuck home.

Infuriatingly enough, his hands gently wrap around my fists instead, and hold them still against him.

"I didn't know." His face is genuinely confused. Kalen looks around as if any of these hybrids will provide an answer he doesn't have. "I thought— I don't know, I assumed that you had volunteered. Or that you and Knox had a deal of your own. I even wondered if maybe your business had fallen through. Knox and I agreed on a plan that never involved you," he confirmed. "Makes no sense to put you in the middle of it ... even if it's taken longer than the original timeline to work things out. Involving you was too high a risk."

He turns away, grabbing my hand to follow him as he continues to talk to himself. I pull away, backing up.

"Mel," he growls. "I'm not leaving you here."

"Like hell am I going with someone who just put my life on the line."

"I said I didn't know," he insists through gritted teeth. "But even if I did and you hated me for it, that wouldn't matter. I refuse to abandon you in this compromised prison run by a man who employs *torture*. I trust no one else in this facility to ensure your safety except myself. So, after we leave here, if you refuse to listen to me, that's your choice. But you are leaving this place with *me*. Your safety isn't up for debate."

"Oh, *now*, my safety matters," I reply, my voice dripping with sarcasm. Inside, in some feral part of me, his protectiveness is that much hotter. I blame the pheromones he accidentally released into me earlier through one of his spikes.

Kalen says firmly. "Why do you think we took you in as our personal chef? You think it was just for your cooking skills? Your father left you without a thought. In The Divide, we see each other as family. We protect each other. I wanted to keep an eye on you, so I made you work closely with me. I had my foot soldiers acting as your private security."

His confession catches me off guard. I hate that it makes sense, and that the thought of him caring about me makes my throat dry. I want to continue being mad, but I'm not sure I can even muster up the strength it requires.

"Come on," Kalen says again, hand outstretched, and this time I clasp it.

"Stop!" yells a voice over the sirens. Kalen and I whip around towards the source of the sound. It's Dirk and another man - a guard. Dirk has a gun trained on us, slowly walking forward.

We freeze. I take a chance and turn towards the direction we had been heading to make our escape, but to my horror, two other figures are approaching us from that end. They're guards too from what I can make out. Kalen's looking from Dirk to the guards as if deciding who poses the greater threat and mentally deciding who to protect me from. I hear the growl rumbling in his chest.

Dirk continues his approach at a walking pace with his gun pointed at one of us, and then the other. Kalen carefully moves himself in front of me, and pushes me behind him, not towards the guards approaching from the other end, but closer to the wall behind us.

Dirk suddenly runs at us, and Kalen faces him. He cocks his gun.

I open my mouth to call his name, to reason with Dirk, but before I can react, I'm grabbed from behind by a claw-like arm. It scratches my skin as it yanks me so hard that I hear a *pop*.

I scream.

Fresh, hot pain radiates up my shoulder from where it's probably dislocated. The same arm that yanked me slips up until it's around my neck, pinning me to a chest that's too tall to belong to a regular human. Instinctually, I reach for the forearm, but pause as a stinging pain shoots through my shoulder. I try and fail to stifle the whimper that escapes my lips. Craning my neck, I look up at my captor. Sure enough, it's not a human man, not entirely. Like Kalen, he's a hybrid, but there's something off about him. His eyes are especially unsettling – wide open with dilated pupils imparting a wild look. His fangs are bared and saliva drips from the tips.

"Be still," Dirk snaps as I squirm. I pull my focus away from my captor and toward Crowe. Not Kalen, but *Crowe*, because all the gentleness in his face is gone, replaced by an anger I've never witnessed in him before.

Despite his grimace, he's disturbingly calm in demeanor. Yet, one can feel the rage radiating off of him in waves as his eyes remain fixated on my captor. He's a truly intimidating presence, and I see now, why he earned his place as the leader of The Divide.

Wordlessly, Kalen Crowe takes a menacing step toward us.

"Don't move!" Dirk commands, wiggling the gun and shifting it to point at Crowe's head. I feel the hybrid's grip on my neck tighten. "Wouldn't want anything to happen to Melly there, now would you, prisoner 1838?"

"Knew you were an asshole," I manage through a compressed throat. The hybrid male tightens until I wheeze. Crowe's growl sends a shiver up my spine. He looks stronger and more menacing than ever before. He stands tall and broad-shouldered; the scales on his body each have a sharp spike that is raised to full height. His fangs are bared, and his head is tilting downwards slightly, as though he's ready to use his horns if need be.

A surge of hope sweeps through me.

Then I remember it's four against one, and fear begins to trickle in.

"Good work," Dirk says to the male hybrid behind me. "Your first major mission and you executed it well. The warden will be pleased with how much you've progressed through the training."

"Training?" repeats Kalen Crowe, head turning slowly towards him.

Dirk's eyes shift to Crowe, and he scowls. "You're something else. Trying to play hero by thinking you can lead some *epic* prison break? Well, given your ... imminent situation, I guess there's no harm in indulging your curiosity. Yes, this young man went through training very similar to yours."

"So that's what you're calling *torture* and *murder*, now?" Crowe ground out, razor-sharp fangs bared at the man.

"Merely a means to an end," said Dirk, dismissively. "You see, you mutants are part of our prison's new program. We're not just containing you; we're harnessing what you are, refining it. Human-alien DNA allows your kind a goldmine of abilities. But you lot? You squander it on petty crimes. Meaningless shows of power. It's a shame, really. So we aim to direct your kind to something much more important."

My eyes widen.

Kalen Crowe snarls. "And what might that be?"

Dirk chuckles, a cold glint in his eyes. "We've figured out how to turn mutants into an unstoppable force. An army of compliant, powerful fighters, entirely under our control, ready to quash any uprising from your own kind. A mutant police force designed to suppress mutant criminals in this city, with a level of ruthlessness only *your* kind could achieve. And the best part? They're so reconditioned they don't remember an ounce of their former selves. Maybe we'll even take this program countrywide."

Crowe's muscled body strains, and he clenches his fists as though straining not to attack Dirk. The guard next to Dirk nudges him, drawing his attention to the fact that while we've all been distracted, the hybrids have gathered around us like a barricade.

One meant to trap the guards and their hybrid soldier in.

Crowe must notice as soon as Dirk does because he lunges for me. At the same time Dirk goes from aiming his gun at Crowe to aiming it at my head. It all happens too fast for my mind to register, but I'm shoved, and something sears across my temple and forehead.

Then, I'm blinking at the dirty concrete floor, watching a stampede of feet moving around me like water. It's strange how all I can see are feet and the flash of red light. No sound. My head is pounding and something is leaking into my left eye, obstructing my vision. It seeps down my cheek and over my lips – blood.

I notice the feet are getting closer to me, like I'm in the way. Like they're going to go through me to get to whatever is behind. Then I'm scooped up by strong arms that lift me onto a shoulder that looks a lot like... *the spikes*... my brain panics. I don't want to be impaled on Crowe's body. But the spikes are absent. Only soft scales cover his shoulders.

"Almost there, Mel." I feel his voice before I hear his words, the rumble of them traveling from my stomach to my brain. "I've got you."

At this, I relax.

My body slumps down onto Kalen's with exhaustion.

Desperation.

Pain.

The throbbing in my shoulder intensifies, and my headache pounds. Nevertheless, I turn to look behind us, where a throng of hybrids has emerged.

They're closing in on the guards and their brainwashed fighte r...

Chapter 10 – Kalen

I didn't expect breaking out of prison to be a cakewalk, but seeing Melanie at the mercy of that hybrid and then having Dirk shoot at her weren't things I had planned for. Her arm is a hot brand against my body. Broken? Dislocated? It's hard to tell until we get back to my place. The scent of her blood in the air has me on edge, barreling through the other hybrids toward the loading dock.

A sudden boom rocks the foundation, tilting the world around us as dust and rock rain down from above. *Knox's handling his end.* To call my brother unstable would be like calling rain wet. It's simply understood. I love him, but he's chaotic, and where I take after our mother, he takes after our father. The thought drives an involuntary shudder up my spine. It's invaluable when it comes to controlling my Divide enforcers. It's borderline perfect for wet work. But for things that require finesse?

He never met an agreement he couldn't dismantle or an ego he couldn't provoke.

Mel groans, and a moment later, she collapses into me, her full weight drooping over my back like she's asleep. No one in their right mind would sleep at a time like this, so she must've lost consciousness. *Shit*. I have no idea how bad her head injury is. I shake her hard.

"Mel!"

No answer. I'm running before I even comprehend it, bursting through the crowd in the loading dock. I hardly hear the fighting over the sound of Knox's getaway vehicle purring nearby. I'd recognize the engine anywhere because it's *mine*. The bastard drove my damn car to start a prison riot?

I'm near the corner when I spot the Veloc from earlier. Our eyes lock over the fighting and he nods, the only confirmation I get that he's going to honor our earlier agreement and lead as many as he can back to The Divide headquarters. Throwing a quick glance around, I see the guards are mostly gone. Either knocked out or dead. In the distance, new sirens are kicking up. Police from all over the city will be here within minutes and Mel can't be here for it.

Shoving us around the corner, I spot Knox with a guard on the ground, whispering something into his ear before a blade goes through his throat.

"My fucking car?" I haven't seen my brother in at least a month but that's all I can think to say. He throws a grin over his shoulder, opening his mouth to say something I'm sure is meant to piss me off. But he spots Melanie first, and his brow crinkles.

"Why do you have the damn cook over your shoulder?" He eases off the dead man below him and stands. Tucking the blade back into its sheath, he nods in her direction. "Guess the pep talk last night helped. Come on, we gotta go before the police and Commissioner gets here."

The what?!

I don't speak. Can't speak. Because it's taking everything I have not to react to my brother putting my mate at risk, knowingly sending her into danger. At the time he wouldn't have known she was my mate but even as a normal human, Mel didn't belong in this position. What if something had happened to her?

And what the fuck kind of pep talk happened? Was he responsible for the bruise marks on her neck? Carefully, I fold myself into the backseat and settle Mel into the curve of my body. From there, I can see the scorched, bleeding skin from the graze wound and her dislocated shoulder. My claws curve into the backseat as I imagine going back to rid the guard of his throat.

"The fuck?" Knox says over the engine revving. All around us, people are jumping out of the way to avoid the car. "Care to share what the hell happened while you were gone that you now have our cook in your lap?"

"*Chef,*" I growl. "Stop saying fucking cook. She earned a culinary degree and started her own restaurant. Show some respect."

"Okay... now I'm really confused, K." Thankfully, his confusion doesn't keep him from driving, and we're halfway home before I can manage more words.

"A Veloc will be bringing as many as he can to our compound. I've already got an enforcer ready to greet them, but make sure everyone is ready for guests."

A nod and then, "So we're just ignoring the rest? You have her cuddled like a damn mate." He laughs as if it's absurd. The growl that fills the car is threatening, and he wisely closes his mouth, throwing a bewildered look over his shoulder. His eyes are back on the road before I can bark out the demand.

I'm thankful for the short ride through the backstreets of the city because the longer I smell Mel's blood, the less control I have. And my thoughts are muddy.

"What kind of pep talk did you give her?" I ask, my voice mirroring my darker emotions to *protect* her from everything and everyone, even my brother, if need be.

He shifts uncomfortably, the first sign that whatever happened will not be something I want to hear.

"She was taking a while to locate you... and I'll admit I was a little concerned when it took a week, then two," his eyes flash up to the mirror, his eyes filling in, *then four*. "So yeah, I might have rushed things along yesterday."

"Why was she even *there,* Knox? We had a plan. It didn't involve our chef at all." My grip on Mel grows too tight, and I'm glad she's unable to feel it.

"Oh, come on," he sighs. "You think I'd leave you inside that prison indefinitely? What if something went wrong? Cameron's dead. A prisoner confirmed he died in their damn Ice Room experiments."

My stomach recoils as if I've been gut-punched at his words. We had a feeling that our business partner and friend was gone, but hearing it confirmed hit harder than I was prepared for.

This damn place. That warden...

"What if you weren't able to keep to the plan and escape?" my brother continued, bumping me out of my thoughts. "There was no one else I could slip into the prison workforce when I couldn't get eyes on you, Kal. It had to be her. 'Sides, she *owes you,* anyway."

His words settle in the air between us like ash. "And her neck?"

Knox's face is confirmation of what I already know. The shame, and the subtle twitch of his right hand on the wheel as he pulls the vehicle into the indoor car saloon of my luxury estate. For everything we've endured, I've never understood how much he took after our father. His temper. His mood swings. His erratic behavior.

"Listen, I'm not proud of —"

"Knox, I'm going to head inside with my mate, and you're going to shut the fuck up. If I hear even one word, I won't be able to control what I do. My instincts are already demanding blood."

My brother opens his damn mouth anyway, but my words are sharp. "My *mate* has a bruise on her throat from my own blood. I'll handle the offense later when I'm not in a murderous mood."

Then I'm pulling Mel from the car before my idiot little brother ruins the tiny bit of control I have over myself.

To my dismay, I hear the driver's side door swing open and a foot hit the pavement.

"Imma head up too," Knox stupidly announces, "since your place is closer than mine."

I know he's testing me. I cast him a sharp look. A clear warning. He freezes, eyes wide, before carefully placing his foot back into the car and closing the door like he's trying not to anger a wild animal. And in this moment, I suppose, I am one.

"Er, on second thought, I'll swing by later," he says through the window and drives off. It only registers to me then that he's taken my car with him yet again.

This guy, I swear to fucking God.

Chapter 11 - Mel

"**M**el," someone rasps from the darkness of my mind. The voice is familiar, drawing something warm out of my blood. My limbs feel syrupy and thick, still pressed between the seams of whatever dream I had. Sleep is slipping away gradually, and I'm desperate to claw it back, to ignore the significant presence shifting the air around me and how it draws liquid from between my legs.

He strokes my arm and then slides pointed fingers down to link with my own. I'm flushed with the sudden urge to feel those fingers elsewhere.

Anxiety wants to pinch the back of my mind, but I don't want to remember whatever has my mind tense. Not the clawed fingers I can suddenly imagine in my mind's eye. Not the ripped body with dragon-like scales that felt surprisingly soft to the touch, when they weren't turning into spikes... Not the last month of my life that had been stolen and altered forever. Or the cell bars.

Sleep is easier to reconcile, and I get the sense I haven't had enough of it lately.

But then, the heat is rising, drawing my attention out like a stubborn child.

"*Mel,*" Kalen growls. Can he tell where my thoughts are going? Claws prick the inside of my wrist, enough to pinch but not break the skin. That rasp of sharpness only makes my body throb harder, too oppressive to ignore. *I need something to ease it.* It aches and builds, striking like a drum beat with each intake of breath. By the time it makes me crack my eyes open, the heat has become a rhythm under my skin—a second pulse.

It kicks into overdrive, spiraling downward when my vision clears, and he's *everywhere.*

Kalen's face is too close as he peers down at me, claw-tipped fingers smoothing over the gauze bandage on my forehead with concern on his face. I jerk at the action and he kisses me over the gauze in apology.

"Dirk shot at you," Kalen speaks quietly, his tone is perfectly controlled but his face is visibly upset. "I pushed you out of the way in time so the bullet only managed to graze you. Still, it was a nasty wound, and when you passed out, I was so worried."

I'm hardly listening as I move to sit up, but Kalen's hands carefully push me back down.

"I disinfected the wound and wrapped it up. Thankfully, you seem to be healing quickly. But, just relax for now. I'll look after you."

"Mhm, thank you, baby," I say distractedly. I find myself mesmerized by damp waves like silk that fall over Kalen's shoulders and ears as he leans closer to me. My fingers twitch of their own will, but I suppress the urge to reach out and touch.

My eyes trail over his horns. Would he let me grip them while I rode his face? *Down girl.* The direction of my thoughts should alarm me, but I'm too far gone for that. I want what I want. Need it. Like I need to feel the sharpness of his defined jawline rub against my thighs.

This can't be good.

His complexion looks healthier than I've seen it in a while. He's not as pale as before. Now, his color has deepened to its original rich and healthy slate-gray hue, and there is a noticeable blush of blood racing under his skin. His lips. It softens him just enough to make his mouth enticing. Full lips curve into a smirk as I watch.

I follow the curve of his neck to his smooth chest under his shirt. The fabric is thin and made of cotton, stretched across his defined chest and bulging biceps. Just the sight of him in such see-through clothes is enough to make me wetter.

His eyes immediately drop to the area between my legs, no doubt noticing the physical response I'm having. It shouldn't be so tantalizing, but it makes me want to playfully tease him with how aroused I can become until he can't resist any longer. Until he cracks.

I want him closer. I crave him.

He's so similar to his old self, yet somehow more alluring than before. My eyes can't help but roam over his body, trailing down his form toward...

"Your eyes are still dilated," he says, though it takes me too long to understand the words. My gaze is fixed on his manhood until he gently tilts my chin up. The jade pools of his eyes are so *warm*. With each ragged breath of mine, our chests are close to touching. I'm suddenly aware of how clammy my skin feels.

I think I need the friction. I don't realize I'm pressing closer until his hand is forcing me back in place.

Kalen sighs languidly. "Mel, take it easy."

Instead of listening, I start to squirm and hope his fingers will brush something more interesting.

"Stop. It's just the unfinished bond. It can wait, so we don't have to rush this."

My desire is on the tip of my tongue. It ignores whatever logic he poses in favor of what those wickedly sharp teeth would feel like against my slick flesh. *When did I stop being afraid?* He shakes out his hair. "I know what you need, but we have to talk first. Can you sit up?"

"Not with you holding me down," I gasp, my veins throbbing with the thought of that strength pinning me in different ways. Then I remember the bliss of his skilled fingers and wonder what access to the rest of him would do. "What's there to talk about?"

He gives me a bewildered stare, but I'm serious. Sex is simple, isn't it? As long as I don't impale my hands on another spike of his again, what more is there to say? As if Crowe knows precisely what I'm thinking, he snarls, leaning so close his next words brush against my lips. "*This* is not just sex, Melanie. This is our future —both yours and mine. And I don't care how good you smell—" he says the last bit like it's pried unwillingly from his psyche— "I'm not sealing the bond unless you're fully aware. Don't make this any harder."

Trailing my eyes down to the soft, tented pants he wears, I groan at the proud length. "Too late." Maybe impaling my hand on a spike would speed this conversation along. Actually, it feels like I already have.

He glowers and slides away, taking the soothing, addictive scent of his body with him. How can I be so addicted to him already?

"How are your injuries?" He asks. Probing fingers check my head once more before dropping to my shoulder. "You had a strong dose of my pheromones in the cell, and the damage was minor. I gave you another boost when we arrived. But is there any pain?"

Either my brain is still half-sleep, or those pheromones have me in a death grip because as he steps back, all I see is the hard-on he's not even trying to hide.

"Hm?"

"The pain, baby."

"No, no pain ... How tall are you anyway? Over six feet obviously, but like what?" *Smooth, Mel, super smooth.* He was tall and well-built and I've always wondered since I had to look up to make eye contact with him and I was five-foot six. That and the heft of him in my hand was impressive...

He makes a pained sound in the back of his throat like *I'm killing him.* "Six three."

As I meet his gaze, I realize there's only one part of his anatomy that interests me at the moment.

"Which brings me back to the point at hand," says Kalen, trying hard to stay focused on what he seems to think is a very important conversation. His restraint is impressive but it's also annoying as hell. "How much do you understand about Ankylos mates?"

"Specifically?" I ask, sitting up in what I assume is his bed. It's a four-poster bed with beautiful wooden frames and thin, white drapes like something out of a magazine.

My hand reaches for my hair, fingers instantly twisting around a familiar curl. "Not much. But I understand the general concept of a bond meant to tie mates together." I glance around the room to see neat, dark furniture and a wall of closed blinds. "I mean, I grew up aware of different peoples, including hybrids. But I don't know much. Like, I've heard about bonds, but I don't know what triggers them or what seals them, but I can guess."

Kalen's raised brows beg me to attempt an answer, but then drop as if he suddenly realizes what I'll say.

"Se — "

" — No, don't answer that. I mean, yeah, sex begins the sealing of the bond, but there's a specific pattern we cut with our teeth that completes it. I've heard it's different for different species. But they're triggered just as simply. It's chemistry, as far as I know. Our bodies recognize our most compatible match genetically, and then the scent is made to be chemically enticing."

"So, this is all because you like the way I smell?"

"No, this is all because the way you smell makes me want to fuck you through a wall." He admits breathlessly, his eyes glued to my breasts. "Makes me want to take you hard and deep, and etch a pattern into your skin no one would ever be able to copy. All while you remain on all fours for me. Only me."

The desire in his eyes makes me swallow hard.

"And it also makes me happy," he continues. "It reminds me of stew in winter or rain in summer. It's a comfort as much as it's an enticement." He looks away briefly. "I always found your scent enjoyable. It was something that would lure me into the kitchen, making me anticipate some kind of dessert. But instead, I would find you. A different kind of sweet delight. My alien traits were never considered fully functional, not even among Ankylos. And especially not compared to our alien parent race, the Drakon. Growing up, I hid this behind my stature, my intelligence, and demeanor," His bright eyes catch the lamplight as he tilts his head. "But, my traits are definitely functional now. I can feel it."

I frown and reach up to his face to cup his cheek. "Are you really okay?" I ask quietly. Leaning forward, I forget that I'm still angry at being forced into prison. And that I've been betrayed by my father and forced to serve under Crowe like a servant. I ignore all of my body's impulses and the tension between us to focus on how I would feel if the warden had tortured me. Forced me to kill or be killed.

Something passes over his expression.

He leans into my touch. "I'm all right," he begins, but stops at the skeptical expression I give him. "What? You don't believe me?"

"I think you're still in shock and haven't had enough time to sit with everything. What you went through causes people all kinds of PTSD, Kalen."

"Same with you," he interjects, placing his hand gently over mine. "You were shot. You had to clean up after those awful battles. And now you're acting like you want me, an Ankylos. Your boss."

"You think that the reason I want you is because I'm not *thinking* straight?" I ask him, genuinely offended.

"What you've been through causes trauma, too. It's not like you've had time to sit with any of this either, you know," he tells me.

"You might be right about that," I say slowly. "I'm sure we'll both need therapy for this at some point. I already go so ... what's a few more months ... or years, right?"

"How about this? Anytime you decide to address this in therapy, I'll sign up too," he responds, laughing lightly, but he's serious. "I'll even foot your bill."

I smile softly at his offer. "That's sweet of you," I say earnestly. "Thank you."

"It's the least I can do."

I lift a hand and slide it over the taut, swell muscle of his arm. "We may both have some trauma after what we went through and hey, maybe I'm still in shock. But I want you because I just *do*. It's not even a thinking thing to me. It's like breathing." My voice is quiet, vulnerable but I'm determined to let him know how I feel and ease his doubts about us.

He smiles at my words, searching my eyes for sincerity, and my God, he *really* is handsome.

"What?" I press him. "Can't you smell what I think? Don't you know what the thought of running my hands over your body does to me? You can't honestly think my body is lying, too? I was attracted to you the second I saw you in my kitchen that night, and I still feel that way."

He grunts and looks away. "I've always thought you were beautiful, Mel. Too good for me really. Even now, your words are lovely, but I've pumped you full of pheromones again to speed up your healing. I believe *you* believe that you feel this way about me, but that's what pheromones do. They're powerful chemicals. That's all."

I'm growing upset with him as time passes. "Stop!" I snap, irritated. "I'm not afraid of being with you, Kalen. But if you're afraid, just *fucking* say that, and, stop projecting onto me."

"I just don't want you to sober up and feel like you've made a mistake," he confesses after a moment, looking away. Kalen's voice is quiet, as if he's talking to himself. "We didn't exactly start off on the right foot, and things between us went quickly in prison. Plus, after the hell you've been through for the last month, no one would blame you if you wanted nothing to do with me – "

"Things happened how they did," I protest. "It's upsetting. I'm upset," I admit and his gaze shifts to meet mine. I sigh languidly. "But, I don't blame you. You didn't run me into debt or betray me. I don't regret meeting you," I say warmly, reaching out now to play with a lock of his hair, twirling it around my finger. "And please respect my answers. I'm telling you that I want you. I'm not confused, or even inexperienced, for that matter."

That earns me another sharp look that makes me smile. On Kalen Crowe, jealousy looks kind of sexy. He runs a hand over my cheek, his thumb sliding gently across my bottom lip.

"Tell me what happens next," I urge him in a whisper. "I'm ready to be your mate."

"And what happens to the life you've already built for yourself?" he questions me.

I pause at that. I haven't allowed myself to think about life outside of prison work in weeks. Admittedly, I was avoiding it. "My father ruined most of what I built already. So —"

"Consider it fixed," Kalen interjects. "You're fired, and your debt is forgiven. The restaurant. All of it. I won't have that between us. I'll invest in your restaurant to make up for losses as well."

"What?! I — " His words leave me speechless. "Thank you."

"If you want to find your father — "

"I don't. *No*. Leave him wherever he is. Good riddance, but I mean, aside from my restaurant, there isn't much to upend. I live alone, my father was my only family besides some distant relatives. I only have one important person in my life, my best friend, Ally. She's like a sister to me," I say, thinking of her fondly, thinking of how much I owe her for taking care of my restaurant in my absence. A true ride or die. "Aside from Ally, there's no one else," I tell him. "What about you? You have The Divide and whatever your goals are for that prison. Wouldn't a mate disrupt your life?"

There's a softness in Kalen's eyes at my question. "Of course not," he replies, a calm reassurance in his voice as he runs a hand through his hair. "I may have obligations, but that doesn't mean I don't have a life beyond them. My priorities are well-balanced, and my mate would be at the top of that list. Aside from my brother Knox, I have no blood relatives left. Although there are a few people I consider my chosen family. But like yours, my circle is tight-knit."

I nod sharply. "We're the same. So — " I trail off, looking him over once more. "Are you going to tell me what happens next?"

"Next," he whispers before heading to a small cabinet and pulling out some toiletries, "there's a bathroom where you can wash this day off of you." He gestured to the door at the farthest end of his room.

"This your way of saying I'm dirty?"

"I promised you a shower and a strong drink, remember? Besides, what kind of mate would I be if I left you uncared for?"

I followed him to the master bathroom. I instantly found myself gazing around the spacious room, taking in the Calacatta gold marble slab walls and flooring, and the pine wood incense burning on the countertop. "This place is beautiful." I say, and walk over to the large window that provides a gorgeous view of the city below.

I feel a palm on my head, gently stroking my curls. A warm breath brushes against my neck. "My view is better," says Kalen in a voice that makes me melt.

He leads me to the shower, then hands me shower gel, a wash-cloth, and a shower cap before hanging up the towel on a nearby rack.

"Take some time to reset and get clean. Then after, if you still feel the same way you do now, I might be open to explaining the rest. And ... getting you dirty again."

Chapter 12 - Kalen

Why did I offer to make her dirty again?

Now, that's all I can see: her riding my cock. My release painting her lips, her breasts. The way I would pry that luscious ass apart just before I sink home. The way she'd gag around me until she was weeping.

The groan that tears out of me is drowned out by the sound of metal as I wrench the bedroom window open. I need to get my shit together before she leaves the bathroom.

Thankfully, the shower is probably loud enough that she won't hear my pitiful sounds. I can't stop to think about her body under the stream of hot water. There's a cool, flat breeze wafting into my face and it's barely soothing my blood.

Hurriedly, I prepare the bedroom for her return, and take care to have first aid supplies nearby. I fixed her dislocated shoulder while she was out cold, and her head wound seemed to be healing nicely. It will heal without a scar, just like my injuries. I thank the stars in that moment for my alien blood.

My cell phone buzzes and I answer it. It's my maid, Beatrice, a kind older woman who had been tasked with upkeeping my home while I was away. She'd regularly call me in prison on the rare occasion when I was given phone privileges. Beatrice apologizes for missing my arrival home, but I wave it off, reminding her there was no way she could have known. She sounds relieved and happy to hear my voice outside the prison walls, and encourages me to give her a ring if I need anything.

I thank her before hanging up. Then I take a moment to feel utter gratitude for the people in my life. My house staff, my mafia family – I'll be in contact with them soon enough - Knox, and now, Melanie.

I'm truly blessed. It may not always feel that way, but it's true.

This thought temporarily distracts me from the shower, and the body of the gorgeous woman within it. Key word: temporarily. As I listen to the sound of the water on her body, I feel myself growing hard once more.

I stifle a heated sound, and it dies in my throat. What is *wrong* with me? I palm my cock roughly over the soft fabric of my lounge pants. Once for comfort. Twice because another image of my mate thoroughly fucked pops into my mind. I need to let go and ignore the throbbing pulse at the base of my length. I need to take a breath, maybe several, and release my grip.

I tug it a third time. Harder, and curse into my inner elbow because I hear the shower shut off and the soft sounds of her body on the other side of the bathroom door. I try to count to a hundred. I try to unclench my hands. I try my damnedest to ignore the wetness sliding down the front of my pants. If only I could get my cock to settle, but it's probably hopeless. She's too close. Too delicious. And I'm too spun out.

Mel is my mate. I can't believe I even have one. Nothing about my life thus far has made me soft enough for one. I can try to be gentle, but I'm larger than her in every way. I can try to be patient, but I know what the tight vice of her walls will do to me.

Hell, I couldn't even last five minutes in my cell. Her hands touched my body, and there was nothing I could do against the raging urges. I've never heard of mating being this visceral. I never knew it could be uncontrollable like this.

So raw and untamed that I can't even trust myself to give my mate time to adjust. She'll need it. Foreplay too. Rubbing my hand over my jaw, I realize I might not be in the best state to do either.

Every minute outside that prison is a step closer to myself, but it's slow going. My thoughts are less muddled, and I've already begun piecing together our next steps. The cagey feeling that accompanied prison is slowly dissipating, especially now that Mel is okay. There's no way I can turn my back on what I've discovered about that prison. Was it just that *one* facility? It seemed so, but there could easily be more. Did the Prime Minister know about what happened at ProMaxim?

My cock, however, doesn't care about the severity of the situation. I can't seem to make the erection budge, not when I feel *her* phantom fingers on my abs, stroking over my hard-on like it gave her pleasure.

Concern fills me. What kind of mate can't hold himself in check?

She had been injured, lying on the bed unconscious, and still, my mind couldn't stop replaying the sounds she made as she came. Seeing Melanie open her eyes brought with it a wave of relief and lust. I inhale deeply and try to wash away the primal urges that have been riding me for hours. She doesn't need an alien hybrid shredding her apart as he claims what's his. She needs...

"Will it hurt?"

I turn toward the sound of her voice and freeze. The bathroom door swings wide, and she's all I can see. Steam wafts around her frame as she clutches a bath towel to her damp skin. My inner beast must think I'm a fool for trying to tame it because the violent urge to claim her is worse than ever. I want to fuck her more than I want to breathe. She'd make the prettiest little toy.

Her curls are even shorter when they're wet, I realize, watching the water trickle from each strand down to her smooth collarbones. But I bet I can still grip a fist full of those little strands and force her to make a mess of us both. I could pry the best orgasm she's ever had out of her perfect body. Make her feed it to me like oranges and red currants she smells like.

I'm leaking again, and it'll only take one glance down for her to know it. One-half of my mind hopes she does. The other half is uneasy. *What if she isn't ready?*

"Will what hurt?" I respond, more robot than man, as I soak in her glowing brown skin. I think every bit of blood I need to think has traveled south, and I can't even blame myself. I've never been lucky before, but in this, I'm highly favored. She's perfect. Soft brown skin and pretty almond-shaped, chestnut-colored eyes. Her face is more expressive than she knows. Beautiful and gentle, even though I'm not sure I deserve it.

"When you mark me."

"I would never hurt you," I insist with what's left of my mind. "The pheromones should make it so you only feel pleasure. If at any point that changes, you only need to tell me, and I'll stop."

She nods slowly, looking me over. Her eyes catch on my damp pants until lust throbs hard enough to hurt. I can't let that part of me out.

Get a fucking grip.

"And my restaurant is mine?" she whispers, leaning against the doorframe like we're discussing the weather and not our imminent future. Her eyes say something entirely different, hot and focused on where I'm bobbing between my legs. There's a war raging in my head. Over whether I should offer her clothes or beg her to strip. Over whether I should follow her body language or her facial expressions. Her fingers curl into the crease between her breasts, and one of the battles in my mind is lost. It takes everything not to beg for her. What I wouldn't give to lap the beads of moisture there, to leave a filthy mark on every inch of clean skin.

A nod is all I can manage as I desperately try to remember what a restaurant is.

"No more debt. No more working for you?"

"Everything is wiped as far as I'm concerned. And your business will receive a nice grant courtesy of me too, including your dedicated staff." The words rip out of a primal throat, one ready to make her beg and bend and break again and again until she can't stand it. *Calm down.* I need to remember that she'll have questions. That she'll need explanations. I cannot lose what's left of my mind. I can do this for my mate.

"You'll never cheat on me?"

"*Never.* Mates don't cheat," I growl, far more aggressive than I intend, but she should know how serious I am. "It's unthinkable."

"Will we be together for the long haul? Growing old. Building a life?" Her voice is so quietly hopeful it makes my stomach knot. It occurs to me that while she might not feel the bond as strongly as I do, she's wanted someone by her side all the same. I've never considered settling down, but the bond makes the urge as natural as breathing. I always thought she seemed at home in her independence, and maybe she is, but it doesn't mean she's not longing for something more. For rest. For softness. She deserves it. She deserves all the good things in life.

I think of how her father betrayed her and how, when we originally dug into her background, Knox found no evidence of other significant men in her life. No boyfriends, brothers, or uncles. Those thoughts make my response incredibly important. Mel needs to understand that I'm never leaving. Never letting her go either unless it's truly something she wants. There's nothing I wouldn't do to ensure her happiness.

"For as long as I draw breath. I swear it. It's you and me."

Her sigh of relief is near-silent, and her eyes are shining. "Okay. And ... will you be kind?"

I swallow down every awful thing I've ever done. Every awful thing I'd do to keep her happy and safe. "Always. I'll give you everything. And if I'm not kind, you'll give me hell, yeah?"

She smiles. "You say that now, but you haven't seen my temper. And, you've always seemed fair, but *kind* isn't a word I'd use to describe *you*."

"I'm sure your temper is as attractive as the rest of you, Mel. I might not be known for kindness with everyone, but with my mate, I would never want to see you hurt in any way."

Shaking her head, Mel barely seems to be listening anymore. "Pretty words get me every time." She laughs softly to herself. "So it's settled, then."

"What's settled?" I rasp, losing precious brain function the harder I grow. She doesn't answer, choosing instead to drop the towel to her feet.

And fuck if she isn't completely naked. There's something she needs to know... I'm trying to remember... but she's so damn distracting...

"*Mel.*" Am I scolding or begging? I'm not sure it matters anyway because when she steps forward, her brown nipples catch the low light. Her full breasts sway, and I almost forget to breathe. My mouth waters, following the dip of her soft belly to full hips and neatly trimmed hair soaked in her scent. My claws prick against my bare skin.

"You still don't know what happens next, Melanie." Is that panic? Since when do I panic? Apparently, when faced with my mate still glistening damp and smelling like she needs me. What if I hurt her? What if I fuck this up?

"Explain what comes next. And do it quickly. You have until I reach you," she promises, her eyes blown wide and simmering. My cock kicks forward, drawing a hiss as it rubs against the fabric. She takes two steps, and I struggle to remember what I'm supposed to say. Something about me. Something about her.

"We haven't decided where you'll live," I blurt out suddenly, hoping it will jog my memory of what I *actually* need to say.

"We'll figure out something that works for us in time," she says as if she has total confidence in me as her mate. I breathe a little easier, giving her not quite a smile but something warm.

Clearing my throat, I try again. "And finances ... I do well. You don't have to work unless you choose to. I know you love your restaurant, so if you continue working, then keep all your money. We won't need yours since I earn enough. Even then, I'll deposit money into your bank account biweekly like a paycheck ..."

"*God,* Kalen!" she snaps at me as if I'm unbelievable. I can tell she's frustrated but not truly angry. "You want to have, like, a year's worth of conversations all at once? Or is finances dirty talk to you?" Her smile is silly, endearing, and charming. She advances quickly, so I throw up my hands.

"No. *Fuck.* I — I have a knot!" I shout as I suddenly remember.

She pauses at that, only a foot of space between us, waiting for me to continue. "Seriously?"

"It's specific to Ankylos anatomy, and it helps mates conceive." I blow out a tense breath, well aware of how fast my heart is racing. "It would lock us together while I ... er ... well, we don't have to do that at all. For as long as you want. Or forever. But, I just wanted you to be aware because it's incredibly sensitive, and in the heat of the moment, if you touch it, I might not ... it sounds bad to say it like this, but sometimes instincts are hard to override and —"

"So if you're close to orgasm and I touch your knot, you might not be able to help yourself from forcing it in? You might instinctually try to get me pregnant?" She asks plainly, not in irritation but in interest, sending a catastrophic pulse of blood to my cock.

"Well, I mean, I can't — "

"Show me where it is."

There's no hesitation as I pull myself free of my pants and grip the base. I can't help but give it a stroke because it's throbbing so hard I'm not sure I'll be able to keep it together. Especially not as her scent grows, wafting to me on the small breeze from the window. Slowly. So slowly, I actually can't tell it's happening until it's already over. I release my grip, allowing the blood to return. There's a round, dark protrusion at the base where my cock meets my abdomen. Firm and smooth like a stone, not all that different from the armored plates of my shoulders. Just her eyes grazing it makes the point throb hard.

"Here," I rasp, pointing but careful not to touch the swollen flesh. I'm well aware of every drop of lubricant splattering the floor. The next drop is far stickier, creating a thin line from my tip to the floor. Melanie licks her lower lip, and her pupils widen.

I don't expect her to drop to her knees for a closer look. Nor do I expect her to sever the sticky trail of desire with her tongue, following it back to my painfully hard cock.

"What are you doing, Melanie?" I swallow the sudden lump in my throat.

"Can I?" Mel's looking from beneath her lashes, her eyes low and heavy.

"Whatever you want," I say, feeling a false confidence that goes right out the window at the first slide of her tongue. It's heaven on my cock and hell on my self-control. My hand lashes out before I can stop it, gripping her damp curls until my fist grounds me. Fucking hell, the *feel* of her wet, warm tongue. I fight the urge to shove forward.

Whatever line existed between me and my new primal nature has disintegrated. The last line of defense fell when her knees hit the wood floor. When her tongue slid along my sensitive skin. She gives the pulsing knot at the base of my cock a wicked grin, and I shiver. Her soft fingers find the middle of my thighs, running the soft pads upward until they hit the rigid muscles above my cock. There, she runs her hands over the small scales, exploring the texture of my skin. I'm leaning toward her, panting and desperate to feel her mouth fully wrap around me. But all she does is lap up each new drop beading at the head. There's no mercy as she leisurely swirls her tongue in circles like my cock is dessert, and I'm not sure how I'm still standing.

When she slides forward to engulf the head, my back hits the wall. *"Fuck*, Mel. Are you sure about this? You don't have to —"

She silences me with another deep pull, wrapping her hand around the firm base and just over the knot I warned her about. The mischievous glint in her eyes lets me know she's aware of exactly which line she's crossing.

Chapter 13 - Mel

Sucking Kalen's dick might become my new religion.

I feel as desperate to swallow him as he is to be tasted, with his head tossed back, his horns scraping down the wall over and over again. I hum as I trace my hands over his hips. The feel of his scales is unlike anything else, soft but textured. The way they taper into small, thin impressions as they trail toward his dick is mesmerizing. They remind me of a dragon's, only much smaller. A defined waist leads to shredded, thick thighs, and between them, his dick hangs thick and dripping. I've already seen Kalen's muscular upper body inside the prison; the rest of him does not disappoint.

I drag one of my hands up his tapered waist and across his abs, making his cock twitch against my tongue. His chest rises and falls as he struggles to maintain his composure. He's panting now, and the sound undoes me slowly. Not only seeing but hearing his pleasure build, and knowing that I'm the cause is driving me wild. I feel goosebumps rising on my back, and my own body drips with arousal.

I'm holding him steady as I explore.

He's hard as stone, but a dick that heavy is too massive to remain vertical for long. I open my mouth wider for support, and it bobs against my lips, weeping for me. The flavor bursts on my tongue, and I already need another taste. He's addictive. I feel Kalen's hands tangle gently in my hair as I bob my head up and down in a steady rhythm. My hands grip his thighs for support as I eagerly suck and swallow his throbbing member. Hot saliva covers him and drips down my mouth, only to be greedily lapped back up by my hungry tongue. I slide my hands from his hips back to his firm ass, forcing him forward. *Deeper.* His cock is too large to take fully, but I go as far as I can.

I'm growing frenzied.

My fingers wrap around the ribbing over his dick, supporting the weight as the tip rests against my tongue. His eyes burn a path over my body, even with his head thrown back. His delicious scent is all I can taste, and the veined length is the sexiest thing I've ever seen. I test the sensitivity of the skin there, imagining it pressing against me, forcing me open for him to take.

I *need* my mate to fuck me.

It was a quiet thought in the back of my mind when I first woke up, but now it's screaming. It's the mantra on repeat in my head as I slick him down in my mouth, gripping harder, hollowing my jaw to drag moans from him. His face is pinched, his lips open and wet as if he can't help but taste something. As if on cue, his long tongue swipes his mouth again when I suck the tip with my plump lips. He curses, roughly swallowing. He's warm and salty, and when my hand grips his knot hard, his length kicks in my mouth, gifting me more of his essence.

"*Mel,* fuck... ungh... *yes...*" His words end with the sharpest growl, and every muscle in my body is tightly coiled, ready for him to snap. I can't tell if I want him to cum down my throat or buried inside me, but I want his pleasure just as badly as my own. I just know I want *everything*.

Now, one of his hands grabs my hair while the other scrambles to anchor against the wall. His horns continue to scrape against the surface. The wall is probably ruined at this rate, but clearly, neither of us cares. The moans of his pleasure are growing painful and more frequent.

I'm doing that to him, making him desperate and needy to the point of pain. *Me.* His mate. I'm making him pant out my name like a prayer as he ravishes my body with his gaze. The sight of him unraveling above me sets my body on fire, and a primal desire courses through my veins. Before I know it, my fingers instinctively reach for my nipples as I work him over, losing myself in the moment.

Maybe I should have seen it coming, but I'm taken aback when he suddenly rips me off of him and pins me against the wall. I glare at him in frustration. "I wasn't finished yet."

"If I let you keep going, I'll finish first," he mumbles, palming the soaking length I need. Stickiness presses from his tip to my stomach, so warm and wet that my back arches. I lick my lips, and before I can put my tongue away, he's dipping back in for another taste. The softness from Kalen earlier is gone, replaced with a punishing grip over my thighs. Pinpricks of claws sink as far as my skin will allow.

His hot breath tickles my lips as he whispers, "You're mine." I watch as his long tongue slides over his lips once again. I can only nod shakily in response before his lips crash onto mine. The roughness of his kiss ignites a fire within me, and I surrender completely to his passion. His lips are like warm embers, sending shivers down my spine.

Kalen lifts my thigh around his waist with one of his skilled hands, pulling me closer against him, as he lines up my soaking pussy with his heated flesh.

"I want to ruin you," he speaks quietly into my ear.

He's breathless and wild-eyed with hunger as he pulls back to watch me roll my hips against his body. Then he kisses me. A rough groan escapes him as his tongue glides against mine. Because of his teeth, I can only play with what he gives me. It's like he's slowly fucking into my mouth with the tip of his tongue, swirling again and again until he pushes it against my throat. I choke, and my core gushes. He moans, gripping my hip hard and rolling me forward. One eternity passes—maybe two—before he rips his tongue out of my throat, and I cough. Air floods my lungs. Blood floods my face. And what floods between our hips?

Kalen strokes his hand down my chest, carefully sliding over my heaving breasts, ghosting over my nipples to reach between us and dip into the wet mess we're making. The first touch of his fingers on my clit has my back off the wall. Suddenly, I feel myself being lifted. He tosses me onto his bed, and I'm pressed into expensive cotton sheets.

I find myself feverish with need.

"Kalen. Need. You. Now," I grind out, hardly able to form words, as my thighs slowly open and start to shake.

He runs a hand through his dark waves, only for some to fall back into his eyes. His eyes are intense, but his laugh is gentle.

"I'm sure you can hold it together for a little longer." He teases. It's a bluff. His dick is leaking so badly that it splatters my stomach. Kalen's eyes drift down to my pussy with unconcealed desire.

"So fucking perfect, Melanie," he says on his way to his knees. "Want me to fill you up? Make you cum around my hard cock?"

Obviously. What's the hold-up?

I feel myself clench around nothing as wetness trickles down my cheeks. The groan he lets out makes me shiver. *"I need to slow this down,"* he whispers to himself. Or my thigh as he leans his face there to kiss it delicately. He reaches out a claw to delicately trace the outline of my lips, skirting around my sensitive clit. I can hear the wet glide, slippery with want.

Sitting up slightly, I watch him slide the same claw along his tongue.

"Kalen," I plead. His eyes snap to mine as he slips one of my legs over his shoulder, pushing the other until I'm obscenely spread.

"Yes, mate?" he whispers, inches from my skin. Nerve endings are firing everywhere he touches, and the tingle of anticipation grows everywhere he hasn't touched yet. I roll my hips closer, unable to stop the gentle rocking. I just need to be touched. Fucked. Kissed. I need us attached. Bound. Mated.

"Now," I insist. "Please. I didn't torture you like this."

He hums and kisses my shin, then my knee, and whatever other complaint I have dies on my lips as he kisses my inner thigh. I stop caring about anything else.

"You look so perfect like this. Spread out for me." Each of his words blows warm breath against my sensitive clit. Frustration and anticipation are battling so fiercely that I throw my head back. Immediately, his mouth descends.

"So perfect," he snarls into my skin. His whispered words don't stop, but my own sounds drown them out. He laps at my clit

in slow, firm strokes that make my hips thrust with each pass. And then he reminds me just how long his tongue is, thrusting it inside me.

"Kalen... Kalen... *please*..." I'm babbling now, both hands buried in the sheets while he presses my hips upward for a better angle. There's no way I'll survive the orgasm building. His free hand slides up my writhing form to massage a breast. Each dull scrape of his claws over my nipple causes me to jerk.

He hums in approval, and the vibration makes me boneless, only to wind me right back up when my nipple is tweaked. I'm a gasping, moaning mess, so I don't even register reaching for the horns on his head. But then my hands are sliding over them, gripping them for dear life while I start to ride his face.

He shudders, and his horns twitch in response, which makes me think they must be sensitive to some degree. "Yes," he groans, confirming my suspicions. "Squeeze me harder. Use my mouth, it's yours."

Something feral unlocks in us both as I grind against his skilled tongue. His hand grasps my breasts, following the same tempo as his long tongue dancing over my womanhood. His claws feel close to drawing blood, and it's maddening. Then he's thrusting that tongue deep into me, making me arch and gasp more incoherent words. I'm not sure I remember my own name. But I know Kalen's, and I remind him of it over and over again. I utter it in a whisper, a moan, a desperate prayer.

He devours me with his mouth, drawing me in and flicking my clit between his lips until my orgasm builds, tightening my stomach with each thrust of his tongue. For a minute, I can't think. Then, he hits a particularly sensitive part of my walls, and I cry out. My body feels like it's on fire as he picks up the pace.

"Good girl. Keep saying my name like that, baby. I want to hear it when you finally break," he moans, nuzzling my pussy with his nose like he can't help himself. Hot, sizzling pleasure erupts across my skin, and as he licks tight circles around my clit, I detonate.

"Kalen!"

Everything turns liquid. I'm jerking with shocks of pleasure so powerful that my whole body curls toward him, gripping his horns for dear life.

I die.

For a few seconds, I'm so far gone that my brain shuts down. When I return to my senses, my entire lower body is wetter than it should be, and there's a sharp pain radiating up my left forearm. Kalen rises from the foot of the bed. He's using the crook of his arm to wipe liquid away from his jaw, but there's more glistening over his chest, too.

Why is there so much liquid? What happened to my arm?

His eyes are hooded, making them smolder.

"You drenched us both, baby," he says, licking his lips clean. "You didn't tell me you were a squirter."

"I d-didn't k-know." I couldn't be embarrassed if I tried, not with him tugging his dick so sharply the blood beneath its slate-gray tone, makes it flush maroon. Distantly, I'm aware that the pleasure of release hasn't receded. If anything, my body is amping up; my flesh grows more heated, and my core even slicker. My forearm is burning with dizzying tingles.

"And you impaled yourself on one of my spikes again," he whispers, his voice smothered in lust. When did some of his scales grow spikes again? Presently, some of the spikes on his forearm are protruding. *Shit.*

One knee hits the bed beside my thigh. He doesn't even have to say anything. I'm already pulling my own legs open until there's room for him to settle. I can't stop squirming, uninhibited moans pouring from my mouth. My mind is barely functioning as I rock back and forth. I just need some stimulation, or my body is going to burst.

I still haven't remembered how to speak, but my body communicates enough for us both. His pheromones are impossible to ignore now that they're running through my system again. Maybe they never really wore off completely to begin with.

How long will I feel this needy? I wonder vaguely.

My back arches hard, pushing my chest towards the ceiling. My inner muscles contract around nothing, dripping as I blindly reach for him. The sound he makes as he watches me with those piercing green eyes...

Too bad I can't save it to play again later.

He settles between my thighs, still stroking himself so roughly it looks like it hurts. I don't know why it makes me smile, except to know that it's *my* doing.

"Have to be inside you," he grits, his eyes clouded with want. "You need it too, don't you? Those pheromones made you so *fucking* wet."

I nod frantically, watching him lose his composure. But even with his wild words and the way he's losing control of himself, he hesitates.

"You won't hurt me, Kalen," I growl, reaching down to line him up by myself. "I *need* you. *Now.*"

I expect him to immediately slam home at my insistence but he surprises me by staying in place. Kalen exhales roughly, then runs his hands from my thighs to my hips. His legs are shaking.

"Please," I beg, whining. Kalen ignores me, giving my hips a squeeze as if he can't help it, before palming either side of my soft waist.

"Why are you punishing me?" I sob. I'm unraveling. I can't think beyond the pounding need to have him fill me. I'll die without it. If a small dose of Kalen's pheromones brought me to such desperate levels in prison, this larger dose turns me absolutely feral. I lunge forward, chasing his lips, but he presses me firmly against the bed. I squeal and writhe, trying to get free so I can take him to the hilt.

I feel his hips shifting against the sheets, aching to connect with mine. But he keeps himself just out of my reach. It frustrates me how Kalen holds back, intensifying my longing and desire for him. The colors in the room intensify, becoming almost blinding. Sounds amplify to a nearly unbearable level. My body tenses and shifts, moving as if I'm already impaled on his length, and I whimper. Kalen watches for a moment, then curses roughly.

"I don't want to hurt you," he says as if it explains why he hasn't buried himself knot-deep yet.

For a moment, I can't speak, shivering with all the words my lips won't form.

Finally, I manage to find my voice. "You could split me in half if it meant fucking me."

"Shh," he soothes. His hands follow the natural curve over my ribs, and I can barely watch as he slowly draws his fingers over my breasts, nails scraping the skin. "I won't leave you like this."

He's already leaving me like this, letting the pheromones eat away at my brain until I can't tell if I've squirted again. Everything is soaking wet. Am I shaking, or is the bed? My heart is pounding loudly in my ears. The sheets are bunched beneath my fists as he rolls my nipples and plucks, and then his tongue snakes down to flick them. The blunt head of his dick finally slides against my wet heat, and I moan in relief.

I can't wait, desperately thrusting myself toward him, hoping to force the tip in.

Kalen snarls. One hand presses against my neck, not enough to hurt but enough to pin me in place, while his other hand curls into the sheets next to me. I hear the sound of fabric tearing and go still under the pressure as he eases into me. I feel the head of his dick penetrate my entrance in one slow thrust that makes me gasp, only to quickly withdraw. Before I can express my disappointment, Kalen's hips surge forward again, entering me until he's deep inside, filling me up in a way I've never felt before. I moan at the feeling. It's almost painful how deep he is. How thick. But ...

He feels so fucking good.

He leans down to bury his face in the crook of my neck. "Inhale. Exhale," he tells me.

It's then that I realize I've been holding my breath and that he hasn't moved since entering me, giving me time to adjust.

I let out a long sigh. Then, intake air once more.

"That's it. Good girl."

Hearing his praise only serves to increase my need for him. I buck against him, and he takes the hint. Pulling out almost completely, Kalen thrusts back into me all the way to the hilt. I almost don't get the time to fully adjust to his size before his pace quickens. I let out a cacophony of whines, moans, and curses.

"More," I moan, delirious, "More, Kalen. Deeper."

His grunt is followed by a slow thrust and a filthy set of curses. "Hhha, so fucking open, Mel," he pants, "Too soft. Too fucking wet." His words become unintelligible as he presses our cheeks together. Vetiver and bergamot - the scent of him constricts my throat tighter than his hand.

My sole focus is reaching the raw, satisfying cadence of our bodies coming together, the pulsing rhythm I need to stay alive.

"C-can't," he murmurs unintelligibly, and I nod in agreement. "Can't." And then he pushes himself into me until there is no separation between us. My moans are painful, ripping out of my throat as he picks up his speed. He pulls back before surging forward once again, and I'm in heaven.

"Yes, please, deeper," I beg, tears wetting my eyes. They stream down my cheeks. "Need it. Need. Nee —!"

He lifts my hips slightly and thrusts into me again, and this time, the angle hits my walls at the perfect spot. The pleasure is immediate, warm, thick, and *building*. I can't move my body, even as it weeps to go over the edge. I scramble to grip his wrists as his thrusts turn brutal and deep. His forearms are normal again, and soft scales cover them so I don't get hurt. However, I don't notice or care as the wave of euphoria ramps up.

I wish I had claws or teeth so I could sink into him the way he sinks into me. The sounds alone are erotic. We're slipping together again and again, the glide sucking him deeper into me with each thrust. It's like my body is sucking him in and refusing to ever let him go.

Kalen throws his head down, clenching his jaw as my legs curl around him so tight they go numb. I can't lift up, but I can shove my hips down, matching his forceful thrusts with some of my own.

There's a scream building in my throat, rising like the tidal wave of heat and pleasure so thick I don't think I'll survive.

"*Dammit—*" he moans, "Good... too good... Mel. Just..."

More fabric tears, and his grip on my throat lessens. He shakes his head and raises his body enough so that I go from being pinned beneath him, to free to ride him as hard as I need.

"You can..." he gasps, "take it. Take all of me." He groans like he's dying. "I'm so fucking close, Mel."

That spurns me on. I take him from tip to root, harder and faster, rubbing my clit against his pelvis until it makes colors burst behind my eyes. All I can see are his lust-drunk eyes. All I can taste is the orgasm barreling toward us both. Throwing his head back, Kalen's hands reach above to anchor into the mattress.

He rips into it.

I grip his horns for purchase, and somewhere in the distance, I hear him groan aloud. I can't stop.

Can't.

I'm nearly delirious when I finally reach climax, pressing my mouth onto him in a frenzy as my soul feels like it's being torn apart.

Pleasure burns my insides, searing me within an inch of my life as I ride an orgasm so rough and thorough it hurts.

Before either one of us can catch our breath, Kalen effortlessly flips me on my stomach. I feel a claw trail along my ass.

"*Kalen*," I say, breathless and slightly panicked. "Wait a sec. I just came. I'm still –"

"– You said you *needed* me," I hear him say from behind, as he cups my ass in a firm grip. "That I could split you in *half...*" I feel him leaning over my back, his breath on my ear, "so long as it meant fucking you, right?"

My mouth snaps shut as I feel my arousal building once again. I look back at Kalen into his lust-filled gaze, and I can tell he's drunk on his pheromones, too. "S-something like that," I reply in a single breath.

He backs up enough so we can reposition ourselves. I get on my hands and knees, and Kalen gets behind me, spreading me and lapping up my juices. My body twitches, overstimulated, yet Kalen's tongue makes me bite the sheets, feeling my body become wetter once more.

"You're so sweet," he tells me. "I'd go down on you forever if I could."

"Mmm," comes my muffled reply into the sheets. My mind is foggy. I'm a drooling mess. My face and neck are burning with a blush deep under my skin. I feel him kiss my shoulder blade as he lines himself up and thrusts into me, fucking me into the mattress at a punishing pace that hits my sweet spot over and over again. I feel an orgasm building up again.

He leans over me so he's close to my ear.

"Want me to breed you, baby?"

I nodded, hardly registering his words. Just wanting him to keep fucking me. Kalen grunts above me, his hips still moving in a steady rhythm as he pounds into me. Suddenly, he pauses, and I feel my walls stretch further. It's then that I realize what's happening.

No way.

My eyes widen in shock, and I gasp as I feel Kalen's knot growing within me. It stretches my walls, filling me up completely. I try to focus, my mind still reeling from the intense pleasure.

"Kalen," I gasp, struggling a little. But he only grunts and pins me down with his weight.

"Don't worry," he says between panting, "it won't last long. Breathe."

He leans over me and kisses my neck as his knot swells even more, locking us together. I can feel his knot pulsating against my walls. The sensation is intense. Almost too much for me to handle, but it feels incredibly good.

My hands grip the sheets tightly as I try to adjust to this new feeling.

"Fuck," Kalen grunts above me, his hips still moving in a steady rhythm. "You feel so good, Mel."

My mind is a haze of pleasure and desire as I moan, unable to form any coherent words in response. All I can focus on is the way his knot fills me, and how it hits all the right spots as it swells.

"Kalen," I say breathlessly. "I'm so close... Gonna cum... please. Please." I don't even know what I'm saying. I'm babbling as needy tears fill my eyes and run down my cheeks. I taste them on my tongue as I'm filled in a way I've never been before.

"*Come*, then, my mate."

Almost instantly, his words trigger my release. My body tenses up as an orgasm washes over me, and then another. My vision blurs while waves of ecstasy crash through me.

My fluttering walls push him over the edge. "Mel," Kalen moans before he spills himself inside me in thick, hot ropes.

Distantly, I can feel his knot beginning to shrink. When it subsides enough, Kalen pulls out of me slowly, carefully. I'm trembling as the muscles all over my body continue to spasm sporadically.

He lies down and guides me gently to lay beside him, wrapping his muscular arm protectively around me. Shyness suddenly overcomes me as I rest my head against his chiseled chest.

"Mel," he whispers in a soothing voice, his fingers twirling through my short curls in a relaxing way. "Are you okay?" His concern and affection only add to the butterflies in my stomach.

"Yeah, but I may not walk right for a little while."

He chuckles, and I feel the vibrations of his laughter against me. "I tried to warn you about my knot." A pause. "Did - I hurt you?"

"No!" I assure him earnestly. "I'm a little sore, but you didn't hurt me." I shift slightly before realizing, "Shit! You came in me." The words leave my mouth before I can stop them. "Kalen," I turn to him, panic clear in my eyes. "I'm not ready to be a m -"

But he cuts me off with a calming rub of his thumb over my shoulder." - hey, it's all right," he says with a light laugh. His tone suddenly grows more serious, "I – I can't get you pregnant," he confesses.

I shift to stare at him, not comprehending. "What do you mean, Kal? Ankylos are part human, so why wouldn't it be possible?"

"It's not that it's completely impossible," He starts again, "but for whatever reason, our Drakon DNA makes natural conception with full humans incredibly difficult. It's over 99% unlikely without the help of IVF. And even then, it's an intensive feat. It's a curse for some interracial couples when they learn about this, but for others, admittedly, it's a blessing."

It's truly a blessing in my case. I let out a sigh of relief, relaxing against him once more. "That's good to know. *Really* good."

A conversation I once had with Alice suddenly comes to mind. She's in the fetish community, and one night at my apartment, over drinks, she casually told me about a surprise outing her girlfriend had brought her on. She was dragged to a sex club where humans and hybrids met strictly for sex. These full humans had developed a kink for hybrids. The appeal was that they could use hybrids' bodies to indulge in their deepest desires – fucking, breeding, or being bred by them – seemingly without any "real" consequences since conception was next to impossible and hybrids were immune to most transferable human viruses and diseases.

I remember being shocked to learn about the existence of such a place, but now, as I grow closer to Kalen, the existence of these clubs completely sickens me. Hybrids are still people, and they deserve to be treated as more than objects of fetish.

My eyes flicker up at Kalen. I didn't mean to offend him, and I'd never reduce him to a plaything. "Kalen," I speak up, "It's not like ... I'd never consider it ... a baby ... with you. It's just -"

"Hey," he says softly, his voice tired, sexy. "It's not something we need to concern ourselves with right now." His smile is kind. Understanding. "We're just getting to know each other as it is. Children can come later. Or, they may not be in the cards for us. It's okay to go one step at a time. 'Sides, I need more time with you all to myself," he says, squeezing my waist for emphasis. "I owe you some luxurious dates and good memories to override the awful ones from ProMaxim."

"I don't think memories work that way," I say with a half-smile, brushing loose strands of hair from his brilliant green eyes. "But, I appreciate it. Making good memories with you is something I want too."

He smiles and kisses my cheek. "I'd love to stay here like this, but I don't feel like sleeping in wet spots." He stands up and turns away from me. "C'mon, let's wash up, and I'll change the sheets."

"If we keep going like this, you'll have to change the whole mattress," I say and playfully smack his firm ass. Surprised by the gesture, he whips around with a mix of a scowl and a smile on his face. For a moment, there's a tense silence. Then, we burst out laughing.

As much as it sucks to leave the comfort of his bed, we drag ourselves to the bathroom to quickly freshen up. Kalen replaces the linens, and when we finally crawl back into bed, we snuggle together once again.

Kalen reaches for his cell phone on the nightstand beside him and opens a delivery app.

"Hungry?" he questions.

"Starving, actually," I confess, as it occurs to me that I haven't eaten in hours.

"What's your favorite takeout food?"

"Let's both say it on the count of three," I suggest.

He sighs, exasperated. I nudge him. "Fine."

"One. Two. T -"

"Thai!"

"I didn't even say three!"

"Sorry," he smirks, and I know he's aware of how annoying he's being. "Do it again."

"What? Count again? *Why?* There's no point. You ruined it already," I huff, pouting and moving away from him.

He laughs at my childish display and tries to pull me back, but I scoot away.

"Wha - ?!" he starts, incredulous. "Are we having a fight, my mate? And over takeout?"

I lift a shoulder in a shrug, still pouting, playing up my annoyance only just a little.

"For real? *Fine.* I'm sorry. Don't be angry with me. What's your favorite takeout food? I'll get you whatever you want," he says, shaking his phone at me.

I look at him with folded arms and a judging expression, but I can't stay pretend-mad for long.

"Thai," I confess.

He responds, "Seriously?!" And now it's my turn to smirk. "You little brat!" he says, playfully tackling me back into his arms. "I'm getting fried rice and green curry. How about you?"

"Same. Add pad thai noodles, and get some appetizers like spring rolls."

He places the order and then buzzes one of his maids, a kind older woman named Beatrice, brings up bottles of water, chilled wine, and scotch.

"I promised you a drink, remember?" His voice is like velvet, soothing and inviting.

It's not long before our food arrives, and he pours our drinks into glasses as we eat. We spend the next couple of hours cuddling and bonding as we enjoy our meals.

At one point, Kalen turns on the flat-screen television mounted on the wall across from his bed, but neither of us really pays attention to whatever plays in the background. I don't know how it's possible, but I feel so close to Kalen, like I've met him before. Long ago. Maybe in another lifetime or universe. He's surprisingly easy to talk to, and he makes me feel safe.

As if he can hear my thoughts, Kalen samples from his scotch glass and then leans over me. I feel him kiss the top of my head in a chaste, protective gesture.

"Mine," he says simply.

I wrap my arm around his waist, wine glass in hand, feeling warm and slightly buzzed.

"Yours."

Chapter 14 - Kalen

The following morning, I wake up before Mel and get dressed. As I return to rouse her from slumber, I carry a bouquet of twenty roses in my grasp. And I take credit for giving her enough orgasms to have helped knock her out. I know that's the case for me. That, and no longer having to worry about being experimented on, fighting fellow prisoners, or sitting in punishingly cold rooms. Sleeping in my high-end bed and knowing I was safe gave my body permission to fall into a deep, restorative slumber for once in many weeks.

As I approach the bed, I feel a twinge of guilt for disturbing my mate's rest. Mel's beauty is ethereal in her slumber. Her flawless face, delicate complexion, and velvety lashes that kiss her cheeks mesmerize me. Those luscious, inviting lips evoke temptation, and she wears an expression of peacefulness as if finding solace in her dreams. Like me, I imagine this is some of the most quality sleep her restless soul has had in a while.

I glance down at the fragrant flowers in my hands.

Hopefully, the flowers will compensate for some of the inconvenience, I think, as I reach out and gently shake her shoulder.

Her expressive eyes flutter open, grow wide at the sight of me, but then soften with recognition. "Kal —," she starts.

"Good morning, my mate — the most beautiful woman in the world," I say and sit on the edge of my bed, presenting her with an impressive bouquet.

Mel sees the roses in my hands and pulls herself up to a sitting position, shaking her head. She lets out a surprised laugh that warms my heart. I mentally decide I'll always find a way to hear that laugh. I want her to be happy from now on. "Kalen, what's all this?" she asks groggily but amused.

"Roses," I say intelligently.

"Yeah, no kidding, but ... you didn't have to."

"I wanted to. You've seen so much ugliness in the past few weeks alone. This is the least I could do."

"They're gorgeous." She breathes them in, and I can't help but watch her before gathering myself.

"We need to finish the mating ritual," I tell her. "In order to complete the bond. Then ... would you like to stay?"

She looks taken aback but recovers with a charming smile. "I'm not ready to give up my apartment just yet," she admits sheepishly.

"Ah, that's okay," I assure her. "There's no pressure. Keep it for as long as you want. In the meantime, you're welcome to an extended stay here. We've got some nice amenities I bet you'd like."

"Oh?" she said, raising a brow. "Do tell."

"A home theatre, hot tub and lane pool, home bar, personal gym. Even got a lake out back that I like to boat on sometimes when the weather's nice, like today."

Mel whistles at my response. "Okay, you sure you aren't a real estate agent and not a crime lord? Because you're really selling me on this place."

I stifle a laugh. "Crime lord? Is that what you think I am?"

"Well, aren't you?"

"I mean, I prefer 'mafia don' or 'Kingpin,'" I reply, lifting a shoulder in a shrug. "You know, something a little less dramatic."

Mel snickers and shakes her head. "Yeah, because those titles are totally less dramatic, babe," she says sarcastically.

Babe? That's a first. I like it, though. "We'll just have to agree to disagree," I say, reaching out a hand to lace my fingers with hers. They fit together perfectly.

She throws me a mischievous look. "That's a long way of admitting defeat."

I can't help but grin as I lean in close and kiss the back of her hand. "Not defeat, just keeping the peace."

She looks at me with adoration in those vibrant, russet brown eyes. Then, to my surprise, Mel raises my hand to her soft lips and plants a matching kiss there.

My heart skips a beat.

"So, does this mean you're staying over a while?"

Mel smiles slyly. "Obviously."

I look her over. I gave her one of my T-shirts to wear to bed last night, which fits like an oversized tee on her. It's endearing. "I had Beatrice wash your clothes for you," I tell her. "They're on the dresser. But you're gonna stay here for a while. You'll need more."

"Can we stop by my place? I can pack a bag. Plus, I should contact Ally."

"Yeah, sounds good. We can head out soon after you get ready."

She nods eagerly. "About my clothes, please thank Beatrice for me. She works hard."

"She's a lifesaver," I agree. "Held this place down during my absence. That's why I pay her what she's worth. I'll be sure to tell her."

Mel is looking over herself, and before I can ask what's wrong, she speaks up.

"Do I get to pick where you mark me?"

I study her, and my mind briefly returns to last night. Her beautiful body glistened in sweat and limp with exhaustion under me as I made her cum over and over. I'm surprised either of us has the energy to even move today.

I take the flowers from her and put them on the nightstand so they don't get crushed; then, I slowly remove her shirt and set it beside her on the bed.

"Of course you can," I reply. "Turn around and lay down." She complies, facing away from me. I can tell she's nervous, not knowing what to expect. I never explained this part of the mating ritual to her before.

I spread my fingers over her back, dragging over her ribs and down the crease of her cheeks. I can't help but palm one and watch it move.

"Not any time fucking soon, Kalen, I swear to goodness," she says, voice raising an octave as she shakes her butt out of my hand. My soft groan of agreement settles things for later. "Matter of fact, find me some damn panties because hell no."

I chuckle before grabbing her clean underwear from the folded clothes and tossing it at her.

She catches it and slips it on before collapsing back onto her stomach. I can't help but touch her amazing ass again, caressing it gently, casually. "I may have slept well, but I have no fucking energy for that right now. Keep your hands to yourself," she says. Her tone is light, but it still registers as a subtle warning to me.

I open my mouth to be cheeky, but she beats me to it — "Your tongue and your dick too, Kalen."

The laugh we share makes my heart stutter. It's such a strange sense of happiness that I don't know what to do with it, except lean my cheek against her back. I just want to touch her. Be near her. Connect.

"Alright, I've decided," she grumbles into the pillow. "I want it on my right wrist so I can always see it." Melanie stretches out the arm in question.

"All right. Be right back," I promise, heading for the bathroom with rubbing alcohol and cotton balls to sanitize the area in question.

"Mmm," she sighs, her eyelids falling closed. "That's so cold, feels good."

I palm the side of her face where she's flushed and warm. "If you feel any pain, you tell me to stop."

She cracks open her eyes and blinks, then settles in to watch me. "So it's going to be like a tattoo, but instead of ink, there will be a scar?"

"Basically," I confirm, concentrating on cleaning her skin.

She watches me, contemplatively. "Will I be able to give you one? I've never thought about biting someone before, but I dunno, stranger things have happened lately."

The thought makes my exhausted cock jump, but I ignore it. "My skin's thick, baby. I don't think those blunt little teeth will make much difference."

She pouts, her brow crinkling. "'Mate an Ankylos,' they said. 'They'll give you whatever you want,' they said."

"No one said that but me." I laugh at her mocking eye roll.

"Not the point. Now, I want to mark you! You could start the bite, and I'll just finish it. Boom, problem solved."

"Damn, you want to bite me that badly?"

"I want you to wear something from me the same way I'll wear something from you. Only fair." Her smile is feline and satisfied so I can't find it in me to say no. So I nod and lean in.

"Ready?"

She wiggles her wrist with impatience. The first puncture of my teeth is heaven. Similar to sinking into her heat but different. Yes, it's erotic, but it's more. I can feel her blood pumping. I can taste her scent like it's soaking into me. It's blinding and blissful in a way that doesn't have anything to do with my cock. It's like tasting home: safety, contentment, joy.

I watch Melanie's face soften, her eyes round and clear as she watches me work. The back of my eyes sting, and it's the closest I've ever come to crying, I think.

But as I drag my mouth around in an intricate pattern, our eyes lock, silently promising each other a million unspoken things. It's shocking how much I feel when I stare into her eyes. It might not be love yet, but it'll grow. She's easy to love with her smart mouth and curious eyes, her beauty, her sweetness, her insatiable appetite for life, and her dedication to her goals.

It occurs to me that when I peer into her eyes, I see no fear or signs of worry. She's an open book, expressively hopeful and gentle with me. She trusts me. Moreover, she accepts me for who I am as I accept her. This feeling of mutual trust and acceptance is rare to me, and I know without a shadow of a doubt that I'll never let it go.

I clean and dress her wound, and we spend a little more time just enjoying each other's company. Twenty minutes later, I head downstairs while Mel washes up and gets dressed for the day ahead.

"About fucking time," my brother drawls. I freeze half-step on the stairs.

I nearly jump and turn to see him leaning back in my chair in the living room as if he owns it. He's shuffling a stack of playing cards between his fingers. "So last night went well, I take it?" he asks, his tone obnoxious.

I don't answer.

"What's your plan for the chef anyway? You don't usually take women to bed. For a while I even thought you might be ..." the words die in his throat at the single cold look from me that has his feet back on the ground. A second later, he rounds my coffee table, discarding the game cards as he goes.

"Never mind, it's just ... you plan on keeping her or something? You act like you're her mate."

"I am," I say as if it's obvious.

"So you mean you've - " His eyes trail to the ring of teeth marks scarring my left wrist, and his brows raise in shock before he looks back up at me again. He snorts, then clears his throat. "Mates who've met and claimed each other within weeks doesn't sound all that slow to me. But hey, what do I know?"

I glare. I'm not in the mood to play, and brother or not, we will need to have a reckoning about his hands on my mate. For now, though, I need to focus on our next steps and I don't want him shattering my mating high.

"Exactly, Knox. What do you know? It's none of your business, but I plan on keeping her so long as she'll have me."

Knox and I fight a lot. But he's still my blood, and when he hears the sincerity in my voice, he hesitates for a moment as understanding dawns on him. I'm serious about Mel.

To further prove my point I catch him up on my mate and my arrangements. "I'm taking her to that new restaurant, Asterion, downtown. Then, later tonight we'll unwind by enjoying some time on the lake."

"Oh yeah, I forgot they opened a new one, and it's here in this city. That place is always booked months in advance. How'd you get a reservation on such short notice?"

"I know one of the owners," I tell him simply. "Coop, the minotaur shifter. Remember when our foot soldiers did security for the original restaurant last year? In exchange, he promised to take care of us. We deserve something upscale and expensive after being confined to that shithole prison for so long. She didn't serve time with me, but Mel may as well have with the way you forced her to work there."

Knox perks up. "Well, a nice dinner and time on the lake sounds like just what we need after that crazy prison break. Thankfully, our lieutenant Mason is helping out the hybrid prisoners we released and holding things down at The Divide headquarters."

"Uh ... right. But, actually, I made these plans for us."

"Yeah, us. I got it. I'll wear something nice."

"No, just *us*."

"Oh, me and you? Well, why not? Sure. We should celebrate your freedom."

"No, we can always celebrate another time anyway. This is for myself and my mate *alone.* "

"Without your dear brother, Knox?"

I glare at him for playing ignorant. I'm not in the mood for this. He knows Mel and I need time alone to strengthen our bond. I suddenly move towards him, and my hand wraps around his throat. "Seem familiar, brother?"

His face is full of recognition, but he shows no remorse, only frustration. "This again? God, Kalen. You can't hold this against me forever," he mutters. "It was one time too. You act like I do this everytime I see her."

"As my brother and underboss," I intercept him, "kindly bear this in mind 'going forward, hands off my mate.'"

He's shocked at my strength and can only gawk at me as his hands cover mine, desperate to loosen my grip.

"Got it?" I say, squeezing his throat for emphasis. He sees that I'm serious and doesn't bother with a smart-ass quip. Instead, he simply nods. But I don't let go just yet. "I promised Mel a grant for her business. I'm giving her six figures. And you? You'll match *every* dollar. This is not only for hurting her physically, but for hurting her business when you forced her away from her work for a month without warning. We both owe Mel that much, at least. Understand?"

I squeeze at his hesitance until he's nodding frantically.

"Y-yes! *Okay!* I understand," he gasps.

I release him, and he grips his throat, glaring but not daring to fight me. I'm much stronger than I was before, and we both know it. Plus, as the head of The Divide, and my direct underling, we both earn good money. But, I know how much it pains Knox to part with his earnings when he has no choice. Just like seeing Mel's bruises pained me. Fair is fair.

Ironically, I know he would have preferred if I merely hit him for what he did to Mel rather than force him to give her something he values. That's why I had to teach him a lesson by hitting him where it really hurts: His pocketbook.

With that matter finally sorted out, my tone is lighter, and my mood is lifted.

"Good. Now, the refugees?" I ask.

Knox swallows roughly, shrugging off an invisible weight from his shoulders.

"Some have chosen to stay with us and are already being inspected. They're not the best bunch we've ever recruited, but at least they're capable of doing basic foot soldier work. Other ex-prisoners moved on within a few hours of breaking out, determined to disappear in case the Prime Minister's forces went looking for them. Can't blame them, really."

"Are any of the ones who stayed injured?"

"Nothing major. Most were treated for cuts and a few non-life-threatening gunshots. The Veloc, Arlo, has some broken bones, but he's healing..." Knox reports, and his eyes seem to silently take note of the new muscle on my frame and the increased length of my horns and fangs. "How about you? Just what did they put you through in that place?"

"Perhaps I'll tell you about their little experiments on me later," I say dismissively, moving toward my cabinet to take out a tray of my cigars.

I hand Knox a cigar, and he pulls a lighter out of his pocket and lights us both up. I release a puff of smoke into the air and feel my nerves relax. I'm not eager to tell my brother all the ways a weak human like the warden abused me. Tortured me. Stressed me out mentally and physically until my body changed because of it. I know I'll have to tell him some things in time, but I'll save the gritty details for the therapist's office.

"For now, I need to know what's being said about the prison break," I tell my brother as I walk over to the large bayview window in my living room. "Are they blaming anyone? Is Gunther being detained? How many were freed?"

Knox takes a long drag of his cigar and exhales the smoke from his nostrils, reminding me of a fire-breathing dragon. "That's where it gets interesting, brother. There hasn't been a single broadcast about the escape. Not a News segment on TV. Not an online article. Nothing."

At his words, my brows lift in shock, and my eyes widen.

"Exactly!" says Knox.

"Nothing, you say?"

"Well," says Knox, running a hand through his textured quiff. "There's just two forums I found online talking about the incident. But guess what? They're back-of-the-internet conspiracy websites. No one is taking this incident seriously except a few edgy bloggers. I'd say the whole incident is being silenced. Some of our foot soldiers suspect that the remaining prisoners of ProMaxim were quietly moved. The place is now abandoned."

"I can't help wondering if there are more prisons like that one, with torture being carried out on hybrids beneath them..." I tell him quietly.

"There's no proof of that," my brother assures me. "So far, Pro-Maxim was the only one of its kind. Might make sense considering that the prison is connected to the underground parlor incident..."

"Are you serious?!" I demand, whipping my head in his direction. "Explain."

"I instructed our foot soldiers to research the prison's investors for leads, and lo and behold, at the top of the list was Rodrick Haynes - the elected official you offed- the owner of the illegal parlor."

Realization slowly dawned on me. "So you're saying Rodrick funded the warden's experiments?"

"It's not too far of a stretch. But what we know for sure is that the warden and Haynes had a deal. Gunther wasn't just trying to create a private army he could use to control *us;* the plan was also to rent them out to high-profile clientele, like Haynes and his associates, to protect their degenerate gatherings."

"Knowing this makes me wish he was alive," I admit, "so I could kill him all over again." Knox snorts at this. "Do you know if the Prime Minister had a hand in this as well?"

"Doubt it," Knox says dismissively.

"Has he contacted us?"

Knox shakes his head. "No one from the organization has heard from him. He's either ignoring this matter like he does everything else in this damn city, or he doesn't know about it. Either way, does it *really* matter?"

I abandon the window and walk back to face Knox, rubbing my hands together in deep thought. I sigh languidly. "I wish we had confirmation. I don't like leaving things open-ended."

"Then, I guess it's a good thing," Knox says with a smile, unsheathing a thin blade from his pocket, "that I've already tracked down the warden."

"You - what?! And where is the bastard?" I snarl, approaching him with quick strides.

Knox grins darkly as his hazel eyes grow cold. His sharp fangs are bared and glinting like the claws tipping each of his fingers. He licks the blade. "He's detained in the basement, of course. All wrapped up and waiting for you."

"You could've led with that, asshole," I snap, "Might've saved you from nearly being strangled. Maybe even got your ass a restaurant invite," I smirk.

"With the way Melanie's got you whipped, I doubt it," Knox replies. "But hey, at least all's forgiven now, and we can move on."

I glance at him, annoyed. "Funny, I don't recall saying I forgave you for injuring Mel."

"Hey, if she's gonna be part of the family now, and your mate no less, then I'll be nice. I swear it. You two weren't officially together back then, and our relationship dynamics were different," he reasoned.

Wow. It's rare for my brother to actually make a point that sounds rational. I try not to act surprised, lest that boost his already inflated ego. "Hm," I say casually, "I suppose so, Knox. Now follow me."

I could've openly given him the benefit of the doubt, but I immediately decided against it. *Let him feel guilty about Mel for a little longer.* Right now, all my focus is on Gunther. The sadistic prison warden is in *my* basement. Oh, the sweet irony.

I recall all the forced death matches he helped set up between the prisoners while I was incarcerated.

How would Gunther like to take part in one of those matches for once? Go from spectator to fighter? A cold smirk pulls at my lips at the thought as my claws lengthen, filling with a paralyzing toxin.

I'm gonna enjoy this, I decide. For Keith. For everyone, he's hurt, and for every life he's ruined.

My eyes harden as I slip into my role as the ruthless, feared, and respected crime boss of The Divide, Crowe. I know that whatever truths I pry from Gunther's soon-to-be-dead mouth will help keep my kind safe. And my mate, too.

"Move," Knox grunts, overtaking me at the door to the basement stairs. "I get first blood."

I push past him when we reach the bottom of the staircase and immediately spot Gunther tied up on a chair in the center of the room. His eyes are wide when he sees us approach. He stomps his feet and fights against his bonds, shouting obscenities from behind his taped mouth.

"Like *hell* you do."

I crack my knuckles, reminding myself that this has to be quick. Mel and I have dinner reservations and a peaceful boat ride later, after all.

Author's Note

Thank you for reading The Caged Bird's Delight, my second dark paranormal romance book.

If you enjoyed the story or have encouraging or constructive comments please leave a review! It also helps more readers discover my work, so thank you in advance!

Do you prefer your men, hot, sexy, kind of dangerous and not quite human? Then you'll want to join my email list so you can stay up-to-date on all the latest news about my books, including new releases, sales, and giveaways! Also follow me on Instagram for information on new releases, updates and behind the scenes fun posts.

Let's connect~

www.ingramcontent.com/pod-product-compliance
Lightning Source LLC
Chambersburg PA
CBHW071417300726
48976CB00004B/1151